HELLUVA ENGINEER

SHIRLEY PENICK

Photography by Jean Woodfin

Cover Models: Dan Rengering and Kristen Lazarus-Wood

Contact me:

www.shirleypenick.com

www.facebook.com/ShirleyPenickAuthor

To sign up for Shirley's New Release Newsletter, send email to shirleypenick@outlook.com, subject newsletter.

To all the Helluva Engineers I have known, all of you were inspiration for this book. Go Orediggers!

CHAPTER 1

"*W*ell, shit, that's all I need." Professor Patricia Decatur stared at the email she had opened about the upcoming Energy summit, her stomach dropped and started churning. "Seriously, with all the environmental engineers in the world, they had to go and ask *him* to be the keynote speaker?"

She flopped back in her chair that squealed in protest to the abuse, and closed her eyes, how could this happen? No, she must have imagined it, dear God she had to have imagined it, it couldn't really be true, he was coming back here. She peeked through slitted eyes at her ancient desktop computer. Damn still there, she swallowed trying to keep her breakfast down. This news had just ruined her whole day, even her whole month, and she knew she was going to obsess over it.

She looked around the room trying to find something else to think about. Her office was on the second floor of the geological engineering building, one of the oldest and most loved structures on campus. The wood floors creaked but were a beautiful oak with the soft sheen of time and many feet buffing them, for nearly a century. The windows were small, but they opened fully to let in a breeze, when she wanted one, unlike some of the newer buildings.

She grabbed her water bottle and sucked down half of it, in an attempt to calm her stomach, but her eyes were drawn back to the email, making matters worse. Maybe she could take a sabbatical during the summit.

She looked at the old, tattered world map on one wall of her office. Yeah, she could go somewhere like China or Singapore, on the other side of the world, far, far away from Grandville, Colorado. What a great idea! She'd never been to Asia, they probably had some awesome rock formations to study. A great idea, except for the tiny, small issue of her being on the summit steering committee. She was committed to help put on the darn thing.

How had she missed the discussion on the keynote speaker change? She frowned, she'd known they'd had to change speakers. The one scheduled a year ago, had informed them her doctor had nixed all travel plans, due to a high-risk pregnancy.

The committee had probably decided on the new speaker that day she had the flu, the one and only committee meeting she had missed in a year. It was her own damn fault she hadn't read the minutes from that meeting, but that flu had kicked her butt in a big way. She'd never been so sick in her whole life.

But seriously, him? She had never considered that he might be chosen, which was just stupid, he was an excellent engineer and a frat brother to the conference chair. And men did not have high risk pregnancies and could usually travel on short notice. Dammit.

"Dumb, dumb, dumb." She felt like banging her head on

her desk, but she'd have to move the keyboard, or the student assignments, or her lecture notes, or her rocks, or…

"Were you talking to me Dr. Patricia?"

She startled at the question, so caught up obsessing over *that man*, she hadn't even noticed her grad student had arrived. "No Tracy, I was just muttering to myself."

She looked over at the twenty-five-year-old woman who reminded her of herself at that age. Not in looks, they couldn't be more opposite there, if they tried. Her grad student had short chin length, nearly black hair with purple tips, and eyes of the lightest blue that they looked creepy; almost—but not quite—colorless. Tracy was five foot nothing and curvy, with a nose ring, and three earrings in each ear. She had on a black skirt so short it was nearly indecent, a black t-shirt with all kinds of cutouts, that revealed a blood red tank top underneath, and knee-high boots—that to Patricia, resembled combat boots—but were kind of sexy at the same time.

Whereas, she was five foot six with almost no curves, blonde shoulder length hair, gray-green eyes and no piercings except for one in each earlobe. She wore a conservative suit and nearly flat shoes.

No, the way they were the same was in their zeal towards their chosen field. Both of them liked nothing better, than to be out in nature examining geologic strata, outcroppings, and rocks.

Tracy shifted from foot to foot. "So, should I start on the research I was doing last time, or did you have something else for me to do?"

Oh, for goodness sake, here I am woolgathering, and Tracy is waiting for my direction. But seriously, she had no idea, her brain was gone, the email had wiped it clean. What research was she working on? Was there something else needed? She just looked at her grad student and was certain her face was as blank as her mind. *Get it together, now.* "The research is great, I'll let you know if something else is needed, thanks, Tracy."

Tracy walked over to the workbench which held the rock specimens they had collected earlier in the year, that were being categorized and identified. *Oh, right, that research, whew, glad Tracy knows what she's doing.*

The workbench held all the latest equipment for specimen categorization. Her computer might be ancient, but her geology equipment was top of the line, and all the latest technology. She poured all her department money into analysis equipment, she would continue using her old computer until it died. Even if it *had* brought her bad news this morning.

Patricia frowned as she turned back to her email, and there it was—still in black and white—environmental engineer extraordinaire, Steve Sampson, was going to be the keynote speaker at the Energy summit next month. Well, that gave her a whole month to gird her loins, so to speak, and get ready to see the man who had broken her heart. *That jerk.*

It had been ten years—but it still hurt—she mostly ignored the pain of it by staying busy. Busy in her job, and the rec league volleyball team that helped her stay fit and have fun at the same time. Her sister was living in Hawaii so she went out there, once or twice a year, often during the spring and winter breaks. Her brother lived across town, and she joined his family to go jeeping in the mountains, on the weekends in the summer.

So, no, she did not sit around and moon over the one that got away, she was a busy professional woman. She even dated occasionally.

But now he was coming back to their alma-mater, and he was going to be at the summit, here in town for a week at least. She would not be able to avoid him completely, but she would do her damnedest to try. When she did have to see him, there was no way he was going to be able to guess her thoughts and feelings, those would be buried so deep he would need a seismograph to see them.

She stared sightlessly out the window in her office, not seeing the trees just starting to bud, in preparation for spring. Not seeing the cloudless blue sky and the bright sunlight. Not seeing the kids walking between classes.

All she saw was the past and the love they had shared as young adults. Both of them, so full of life and confident they would be together always. But that's not what had happened, now was it.

She grimaced and turned back from her musings. She needed to tell someone, to vent, at least for a minute, but who.

She texted her sister, Diane.

Patricia: Guess who the key note speaker is at the summit. Steve, that's who.

Diane: THE Steve? Oh my God, did you know about that?

Patricia: No! I missed that meeting I guess.

Diane: Do you want me to fly in and run him over with a rental car?

Patricia: LOL No need for violence, I can deal with it.

Diane: OK I'll call tonight after work and we can commiserate. The kids are going to the beach with Kalani so I'll have time.

Patricia: That would be cool, TTYL

Diane: Get some ice cream before I call or wine or a margarita. Definitely a margarita!!!

Patricia: LOL

Diane might have some good advice there—but which

one—ice cream or booze? Hmm, tough choice. She shook her head and went back to work, carefully closing the dangerous email and looking at her to do list.

STEVE SAMPSON CAUGHT HIS REFLECTION IN THE GLASS AND found himself smiling again, he'd been going around grinning like a fool for weeks now. Ever since his frat buddy, Jamal, had called him and asked him to be the keynote speaker at the energy summit his college was having next month.

He hadn't been back to campus in ten years, so going back would be fun and he certainly had plenty to share with the industry professionals, young engineers-to-be, alumni, and department heads that would be attending the weeklong meeting.

But the main reason he found himself grinning like a fool, had nothing to do with that, or his success in his chosen field. No, the real reason he had this sappy expression on his face, is that he had high hopes he would be able to see and talk to his college sweetheart, Patsy. When Jamal had called to ask him to be the keynote, he was glad to agree to do it, but he'd casually asked a few questions about the committee.

He tapped his pen on the ergonomic cordless keyboard in front of him, and stared sightlessly past his dual monitor workstation. His gaze landed across the room on the conversation area he had in his office, to talk to clients.

He knew Patsy was still a professor at their college, he saw her name and picture in the alumni magazine every month, and yes—he could admit it—he always looked. Her picture enthralled him, her blonde hair fell in a soft wave to her just past her shoulders. Her gray-green eyes seemed to stare into him, and he wondered what she was thinking. She had a long nose and a sweetheart mouth.

She still went by her maiden name, that didn't necessarily mean she wasn't married, a lot of professional women kept their maiden name, and for a professor that was even more common, but it didn't keep him from wondering if there was any chance of a reconciliation. Or at the very least if they could be friends.

Hell, who was he kidding, he still loved that woman, and it didn't matter if he hadn't seen her in ten years. He'd picked up the phone a hundred times since his divorce to call her, but fear of her being married had stopped him every single time except once, and that time a man had answered the phone. He hadn't said anything and had just hung up, he'd never tried to call again. She was too beautiful and special to not be married, but he just couldn't squash the hope that she wasn't. Now he would find out for certain.

As innocently as he could, he'd asked about the committee, and Jamal had confirmed she was on it. His frat brother had seen right through his innocent attitude, and had teased him, just a little, about his interest. He hadn't wanted to ask Jamal any other questions, and seem like a desperate fool. But he knew he would at least see her.

Whether she would speak to him was a completely different matter. He'd broken her heart—he knew that—but at the time, he'd thought he was doing the right thing. It hadn't taken a half dozen years before he realized he'd sacrificed himself, and real love, for a woman who didn't appreciate him and wasn't faithful. But hindsight, was a bitch, in his opinion.

His ex-wife, Katerina, was one too. She'd been so sweet and vulnerable ten years ago, and he'd felt like he was the one to help her through the horribly difficult period she was going through. But pity is not the same as love, even though it had felt that way back then. And she hadn't loved him either, she'd just needed a protector and someone to count on.

Once she'd gotten back on her feet, the cheating had started, and she'd kicked him to the curb. But that was four years ago, he'd moved on from that episode in his life, so he was more than ready to see Patsy again. He owed her an apology and an explanation, he wanted, no needed, to see her face and hear her voice, even if it was her yelling at him. He was clearly insane, but maybe after the trip to Colorado he could regain his sanity.

He turned in his chair and ran one finger over the volumes of alumni magazines in the bookshelf behind his desk. So, he was going back to his alma mater, and he hoped he could at least get Patsy to talk to him long enough to explain, what had happened, and get some closure.

Because he still felt bad about how he'd treated her, and he still yearned for the love they'd had. It had been so powerful and so honest, free and a little wild, it was a connection he'd never felt again with anyone else. How had he been so stupid to give that up… he groaned and shook his head at the choices he'd made.

His assistant knocked on his door and stuck his head in, just as the computer dinged to remind him of the meeting he had in five minutes. He put aside his musings about the past —and what might happen next month—picked up his laptop and cell phone, to join his assistant, as they started toward the conference room.

He still had a whole month to get through, before he would be heading to Colorado. He just hoped he wouldn't build up too much expectation.

CHAPTER 2

$\mathcal{S}$teve smiled as he drove into Grandville, he hadn't been back to campus in years. It was a gorgeous campus with big trees and open space, nestled at the foot of the Rocky Mountains. The skies were a bright—almost too dazzling—blue, the sunlight strong in the high altitude.

The trees were starting to leaf out and flowers were springing up in the flower beds. He noticed a lot of new buildings had been built in the ten years since he'd been back. The school must be doing well, to be able to afford all the new development.

There were even a couple of new frat houses. Now that was different, for years it had been the same half dozen fraternities in the same buildings. Two of them he noticed had girls coming out of them, well, well, well, now that was something he never thought he would see.

The ratio between women and men students must be narrowing to support two female fraternities. Some people might call them sororities, but he knew many of the societies went by the original designation of women's fraternities.

He'd gotten quite the lecture on the subject back when he was attending the school.

He chuckled at the memory. Female engineers were a breed of strong self-assured women, even today they were a minority in the workplace and they often felt they had to prove themselves to the world to be taken seriously. So, if they had an opinion on something, you'd best listen.

Some young men were playing Frisbee in the commons, they were so young looking. A couple of them had their shirts off and they looked like young Greek gods, but the girls on campus didn't even look at them. Being surrounded by men —constantly—took some of the shine off them, he supposed.

The freshmen girls were always a little star struck at the beginning of the year, but by the time spring hit they had become immune, and the guys were just their classmates. Some of them hooked up, but it was a hard school, so relationships took a back seat to studies.

When the school had first started allowing women to join the ranks of students, some of the men had said the women were there for an M R S degree, but they'd learned to keep their opinions to themselves, when some of those women scored higher on the tests than they did.

The first year often weeded out the serious students. It was not a school where a person could skate by, even the sports teams had to keep up academically. Which is probably why, even though they had good athletes, they rarely did well against the other colleges.

Studies took the front-seat over sports, and it was such a small school that they didn't have the breadth of talent to draw from. Just to get into the school at all, a person had to be in the top ten percent of their high school and have damn good scores on the tests.

He drove past the campus and into the town proper. He headed toward the restaurant where he was meeting Jamal, they had the best meatball sandwiches, and he was looking forward to the experience again. There were a couple of other restaurants he planned to hit while he was in town.

He hoped he could entice Patsy to go with him, to what had been their favorite Mexican restaurant, if he could manage that feat, he would feel like he was forgiven. The two of them had spent many an hour in that place, they had a Colorado sauce they put on burritos that was better than any he had tasted since, and huge margaritas.

The main part of town was quite the happening place it seemed. It was very trendy, and he'd heard it was the new LoDo in the foothills. Some of the old hangouts were there, but a lot of the stores and restaurants along the main street had been sold and converted. People swarmed the streets even on a weekday. Back when he was in school, the main downtown area had been nearly a ghost town on weekdays, not so anymore.

Parking his silver non-descript rental car in front of the restaurant, he went inside to see if Jamal was there yet. The memories hit him hard. The place looked the same as it had ten years ago, maybe spruced up a bit, but not much. It had the typical Italian décor of red checked tablecloths and wine bottles masquerading as candle holders, with the wax from many candles dripping down the side.

He wasn't sure where you could even buy candles that still did that, but apparently, you could somewhere. There was a salad bar in the corner that didn't seemed to be getting a lot of action. The walls had pictures of Italy and mining equipment vying for space. It was an odd combination anywhere except here.

11

A rich marinara scent wafted from the kitchen, and people around the room had spaghetti or meatball sandwiches or alfredo. He wasn't sure he could ever remember eating anything except the meatball sandwiches. Soft Italian music played from speakers and the conversations around the room added to the sound.

At one table a couple of young men, most likely grad students, had some E4 paper out and one was drawing bell curve graphs with charts of numbers next to them. Steve laughed to himself thinking of all the discussions this room had endured on the finer points of physics, imaginary numbers, and chemical formulas; along with mining practices, metallurgical processes, and seismic interpretation.

He didn't see Jamal in the room; he would probably walk down from campus. The town didn't have the best parking and since Jamal was probably in a faculty lot up on the hill, it just made sense to leave his car there. So, he would probably be coming in any moment.

Steve asked the waitress for a table for two and she seated him at a table where he could see the door. While he waited, he checked his email and sent off a couple of responses to clients and associates, when Jamal still wasn't there, he checked Facebook.

Patricia's desk phone rang with a local number she didn't recognize, so she answered, "Dr. Decatur, how may I help you?"

There was a silence on the other side, then a muffled voice said, "Patricia, Jamal here, hold on a sec."

She heard the phone receiver clatter to the table. A land

line? Did people still have those? It wasn't an internal campus number, so it had to be a house phone. Then she heard what sounded like retching. Oh no, no, no, no. She knew what he was going to ask, no, no, no.

"Patricia, sorry about that. I have the stomach flu, as does my wife and both kids, we are a serious mess here. I hate to ask, but can you go join Steve at the Italian place, he's probably there waiting for me."

"I'm busy right now, Jamal." She looked frantically around her desk for something to be busy with.

"I'm sorry, but you're the only other person on the committee who knows him, and the only number he has for me is my cell, which is currently in a jar of rice, after... well you don't want to hear the rest, trust me. I can't call him because his number is on that phone. It never occurred to me to write it down somewhere. Oh, man, hold on a sec." Again, the phone clattered, and again, she heard retching.

Damn it, she didn't really have a choice in this, she had to go tell Steve what happened. Jamal was clearly sick, and not just slightly sick. Yuck.

"Patricia please, you're my only hope."

She sighed. "Fine, I'll go, but don't start spouting any more Star Wars at me."

He chuckled weakly. "May the force be with you. You've got that extra room too, that will work. Oh, God, gotta go again." And he hung up the phone.

She set her phone receiver down carefully, since she really wanted to slam it. Then just sat there with her head in her hands. *Dear God, do I have to go have lunch with the man? And in one of our favorite hangouts?* Of course, it was pretty much everyone's favorite hangout because the food couldn't be beat, but still.

She thought about hitting her head on the desk, but it was still covered and would take too long to clear off a spot. *Okay, I can do this, it's an hour at most, maybe I can rush, and it will be only a half hour. Sure, that will work.*

CHAPTER 3

*P*atricia walked slowly toward the restaurant, she normally loved eating there, but she was pretty certain that wasn't happening today. Her stomach was in knots, as she thought about seeing Steve again.

She got to the corner of the building and stopped dead, she had to go in there, she couldn't just stand out here like some ninny. What could possibly happen in a crowded restaurant? *Knock it off, stop acting like a dumb ass and get your butt in there.*

She threw her shoulders back, lifted her chin and walked purposely into the restaurant. Her eyes were drawn to him, the second she was over the threshold. He was looking at his phone and didn't see her yet, so she hesitated in order to look him over. God the man was still a fox, his dark hair curled just a little on top where it was a bit longer, he kept the rest short, probably so it didn't get too wild.

Back in college he'd let it grow long for a while, and it had been so curly it was nearly an afro. He wouldn't let it go for long, because he didn't really like the curls. His shoulders were broader than she remembered as he hunched over his phone. She knew his eyes were a bright clear shade of sky blue that sparkled when he laughed and grew dark with passion. The beard was new, it was kept short and emphasized his jaw.

She shivered, nope not going there, maybe she could just back slowly out the door. She could call and tell the restaurant to relay a message. No, she had never been a chicken-shit and she wasn't going to start today.

She shook her head, smoothed down her skirt, and turned to the hostess. Normally when she walked into this restaurant the first thing she noticed was the rich smell of marinara sauce, but that was not the case today. Today it was all about the man sitting on the other side of the room.

She let the hostess know she was meeting him and walked over to the table. As she neared his table he looked up and their eyes met, his seemed to warm at the sight of her. His expression nearly made her falter in her steps, but instead she plastered a fake smile on her face and stepped forward.

He stood and smiled at her warmly. "Patsy—"

Oh, hell no, no nicknames. She cut him off. "Patricia. I go by Patricia. It's pleasant to see you again, Steve. Please, let's sit." She needed to sit now, she wasn't sure her legs would hold her another five seconds.

She reached out toward her chair and he leapt to pull it out for her. He'd always been a gentleman that way, but she tensed, she didn't want him treating her any different than any other colleague, she needed to make sure he understood that immediately. But instead, she just sat, and shivered a bit as he pushed her chair in.

When he was seated, she folded her hands together and said primly, "Jamal called me and asked me to come meet you. He and his whole family have the stomach flu. He sounded really sick."

Steve nodded. "I wondered, I didn't remember him ever being so late, he was supposed to meet me almost an hour ago. Poor guy, a whole house of sick people doesn't sound like fun. I hope they all feel better soon."

"Yeah, he's going to be upset if he misses the summit, he's worked really hard on it." She felt bad that she had dawdled on her way to the restaurant, making him worry about his friend.

"I think the stomach flu only lasts a couple of days, doesn't it?" he asked.

"That's what I was thinking too. Since the actual summit doesn't start until Monday, he should be fine. He could always miss the Sunday night reception. You came in early."

He shrugged. "No reason not to. I thought maybe a trip into the mountains would be fun over the weekend. The hills in Virginia are not quite the same as they are here."

"No, I guess not." She didn't want to think about him and a trip to the mountains, it was an activity she had done with him many times in the past, and it had always been a sensual experience. The man could make camping into a pleasure sport.

They'd made love under the stars. They'd made love in bright daylight next to a stream. They'd made love in the back of his truck. They'd made love in caves and caverns as they explored them. And they'd made love in abandoned gold and silver mines.

Nope, she did not want to think about him and the mountains, but she had, and now she felt flushed. Her body was reacting to the memories, *bad body*. She felt hot and tingly, but she wasn't taking that trip down memory lane, so she reeled in her mind and her physical responses. She hoped he didn't notice, once upon a time he could read her like a book, but that was a long time ago.

17

Thank God, the waitress came up and asked if they were ready to order. They both nodded. Her mouth had gone dry, so she took a quick sip of the water the waitress had brought with her.

Knowing Steve would wait all day for her to order first, she said, "I'll have the meatball sandwich and some iced tea."

He grinned. "I'll have the meatball sandwich and a coke." When the waitress had walked off to put in their order, he looked her in the eye. "Just like old times."

Her hackles rose and she looked down her nose at him. "Is it? I don't remember. I eat here all the time." It was a lie, she did remember, but she wasn't going there, in any way or any form."

His grin slowly died, and she was sad to see it go, even if she had deliberately forced it away.

The waitress returned with their drinks, one of the best parts of this restaurant—right this minute—was their quick service. When he picked up his soda, she noticed he didn't wear a wedding ring. She had to wonder about that. He'd always said he would wear one when he was married. Did that mean he wasn't? Or had he turned into some kind of player.

STEVE WAS SO GLAD TO BE SITTING ACROSS FROM PATSY HE could hardly keep from grinning. He felt sorry for Jamal and his family but couldn't regret that she was here instead of his buddy. She looked so good, her blonde hair was up in a twist and her gray green eyes were stormy.

He didn't think she was very happy to be having lunch with him. She was dressed in a conservative suit of dark blue with a shirt that just barely had a touch of turquoise to it. She had on a slim bracelet with small turquoise stones set in it and earrings that also had turquoise stones in them.

He wondered if she'd collected those stones herself—probably—she loved to go out in the fields and find stones that had come loose from the beds that had housed them for centuries. She rarely used her rock hammer to remove stones from a bed, unless it was for scientific reasons. But the loose stones she felt were fair game and she had a friend who could set the stones for her, into jewelry. A friend of a friend—if he remembered correctly—who lived somewhere in Washington state, or at least had ten years ago.

He stifled a sigh and wondered how much had changed in her life while he'd been living in Virginia. He did notice that she was not wearing any rings, and in particular, she was not wearing a *wedding* ring. He was sure she was the type that would wear one if she was married. His heart soared with hope that she was single and available, what he would do about that from Virginia he didn't know, but he was damn well going to try.

He didn't know what to talk about, there was so much he wanted to say, but he didn't think the restaurant on her lunch break was the time or place. He didn't want to ruin lunch by revealing all of what it meant that Jamal and his whole family was sick. He needed to wait until after they ate, for that little revelation. She didn't eat when she was upset—as he recalled—and he didn't want to ruin her lunch.

She seemed to get flustered when he mentioned going into the mountains, and he wondered if she was thinking about their trips up there, and all the fun they'd had, both clothed and naked. He certainly hoped she was thinking about it. He sure was, and if he didn't get something else on his mind, he was going to be very embarrassed to leave the restaurant.

The summit was probably a safe topic, yeah, they could talk about that while they ate. And that's exactly what they did. It was a pleasant conversation, and he learned a lot about what all would be taking place, who the workshop presenters were and what topics they would be speaking on. It sounded like it would be a great summit, with a lot of information exchanged.

When they were almost finished eating. He took a drink from his glass and as he set it back down on the table he said, "So, did Jamal mention anything about alternative arrangements for me?"

She looked confused and shook her head. "What do you mean?"

"Well, I was supposed to stay at his house for the week, but now I can't. He didn't mention that?" He watched and saw the exact moment what he was saying dawned on her.

"You have nowhere to stay? Is that what he meant by saying my spare room would be perfect? Oh no, I am not playing hotel. No way, no how, just no."

"But Patsy, um Patricia, I don't have anywhere else. The whole town is booked for the summit, no hotels, no dorm rooms, no space in the frat houses. When Jamal called me two months ago, I called everywhere and nothing was available, he finally said I could stay in his guest room." With each full location, he saw her get stiffer and stiffer, until she was nearly vibrating from the tension. If she was a violin string, it would have snapped from the pressure.

"Dammit, I should have let the woman who called me take the room, but I just didn't want anyone in my space for a week. And I don't know her from Adam."

"I'm sorry, but if you look on the bright side, at least you know me."

"Yeah, I don't see that as anything in your favor, Steven

Lee Sampson. What will your wife think about you staying with your old girlfriend?"

Oh man, his full name, she wasn't a happy camper. "I'm not married, we've been divorced four years. I won't bother you, you won't even know I'm there."

She snorted. "Yeah right." She folded her arms and glared at him, he just kept his expression innocent and hopefully trustworthy. After a minute or two, that seemed like an hour she sighed. "Fine, let's get going, I can show you where I live, but then I have a class to teach."

"Great." He took some cash out and laid it on the check, stood and moved behind her chair to pull it back for her.

She swatted at him. "Knock off the chivalry already, I can manage to get out of my chair."

"I know, but my mama taught me to always be a gentleman." He grinned at her.

She stuck out her tongue at him.

This was going to be a great week.

CHAPTER 4

his was going to be a horrible week. She was going to have *that man* living in her house for a whole fricken week, seriously? How did she get herself into this mess? Sitting across from him for lunch was bad enough, she wanted to lap him up and punch him in the nose, at the same time.

He looked so damn good, like a cold drink of water on a warm day, or maybe more potent, an ice-cold beer on a hot day, no still too tame, a frozen double shot margarita? Closer but still not enough. She had nothing to compare him to, he was in a class by himself. Always had been.

And he was divorced, what the hell was *that* all about. She didn't know what to do with that knowledge. Good thing she didn't have to stay at her house, while he unpacked and settled in. She had a couple of classes to teach, so that would keep her mind away from him. She went off to teach her class leaving him at her house.

Dear God, Steve Sampson was at her house, never in her wildest dreams could she fathom that. She had a few minutes before class, so she decided to call her sister to commiserate.

"Hi Sis, how's it going?" Diane cheerfully answered her phone.

"You are not going to believe who is unpacking, in my guest room, this moment, as we speak."

"Not Steve, please don't tell me it's Steve."

"Oh yeah, it's Steve all right. Jamal's whole family has the stomach flu, and he was going to stay with them, they're frat brothers. And everything else is booked for miles because of the summit and some concert at Red Rocks. And he's divorced!"

"How did you draw the short straw?"

She huffed as she walked down the hill toward the school. "I'm the only one who knows him, is the excuse Jamal gave me. Of course, that was about all he could say in between bouts of throwing up. It was not a pleasant conversation."

"Eww, TMI Sis. Well, just treat Steve like a guest, or ignore him completely. Divorced huh? So, tell me is he still a hunk or did you get lucky and he's fat and bald, with a squint and bad breath."

She chuckled. "Hardly, no he's still a hunk, maybe even better than he was ten years ago. Tall, wide shoulders, flat stomach, full head of hair, bright blue eyes, trimmed beard, still got it going on, in spades. I didn't get close enough for bad breath detection, but I firmly doubt it."

"Well, you just keep that distance."

"Oh, don't you worry about that. I have no intention of getting close enough to examine his breath." She shook her head and hefted her backpack back up onto her shoulder.

"Good, gottta run, I have a meeting in about two minutes, keep me in the loop."

"I will, thanks Diane."

"I've got your six, always. Love you, bye."

She was smiling as she walked into her classroom, it was

one of her favorite classes to teach, so her afternoon was looking up, she could ignore *that man* at her house, for a couple of hours, anyway.

STEVE WATCHED AS PATSY MARCHED DOWN THE HILL TOWARD campus, he knew she wasn't happy to have him in her house for the week. But he had every intention of making sure when he left, to go back east, that they had worked everything out between them.

She had shields up, in front of the walls, in front of the barbed wire, in front of the land mines, in front of the moat around the castle. But he was going to work hard to breach each one of those obstacles and get to the real her, hiding in the heart of the keep.

While he thought about strategy, he got his bags out of the trunk of his rental car. She'd bought a Victorian house, probably left over from the gold rush days, it was slate blue on the outside with a light gray trim. The house had a real live picket fence around the front yard, and flower beds that were all dead from the winter. He was a little surprised not to see any spring bulb type flowers popping through the ground.

He saw a bright blue Toyota Rav4 in the driveway, that he assumed was hers. It looked brand new, he schlepped his bags over to it and looked in the windows, in the hatch was all her gear. He saw camping gear, a tent, sleeping bags, a small propane stove, lanterns and a cooler. There was snow gear, chains for the tires, a couple of down filled jackets, hats and gloves, a snow shovel, a snow brush for the car with an ice scraper, along with a bag of kitty litter. There was also fishing poles, a shotgun in its case, a tow chain, a large first aid kit, a roadside emergency kit and her geology backpack that would have everything she needed to go scouting. The woman was prepared for every possible eventuality. It wasn't uncommon for anyone who lived in Colorado, especially if they were mountain enthusiasts. But she carried it to the extreme.

He shook his head and took his bags into her house, and upstairs to unpack his suitcase and garment bag in the room she'd assigned to him. It looked like she had an office in another small room next to his, with a bathroom in between the two small rooms. There was only one door on the other side of the hall and he guessed that was the master bedroom, he wondered if she'd done the renovations, or if she'd bought it that way.

He decided he could ask her eventually, if he managed to get her to talk to him, he needed to take the first step tonight, if she didn't run off and hide. But the first order of business was a shower. Traveling always made him feel grungy and it didn't matter if it was a two-hour flight or halfway around the world.

When he felt human again, he wandered around Patsy's home, it was fun to see what her treasures were—rocks naturally—the woman was a geologist after all. There were pictures of vacations and her family.

It looked like her sister Diane had a husband that was either Mexican, or maybe Hawaiian, based on the beach in the background, and a couple of kids. And there were pictures of her brother with a couple of boys and a pregnant wife. Whoa, they needed a TV set, the boys weren't very old. There were also some pictures of field trips with her students. And some older family pictures.

The furniture was all comfortable looking, in neutral colors, with bright colored accents in the throw pillows and lap blankets, nearly every color in the spectrum was present, but blues and turquoise were the predominant colors. She had a lot of plants that were thriving, and three different bowls of beta fish. He knew they had to be kept separate since they were fighting fish, but one all by itself got bored and lonely, so she had three in separate bowls grouped together, so they could see each other, but not *eat* each other.

He wandered into the kitchen and before he could explore it, he saw her teaching schedule for this semester posted on the refrigerator, well that was handy. She would be in classes until five.

She might try to avoid him after that, but now that he knew where she would be, he was going to be there too. Today was Friday and the summit started Sunday evening with a mixer reception.

So, if he snagged her for dinner tonight, he would have some time to work on some of those barricades before the meetings started. He would really like to get her to go into the mountains with him tomorrow. He needed to think of something that would lure her to do that.

Maybe the abandoned amethyst mine would work. He could always say he needed one for his mom for her birthday or Christmas, and it wouldn't be a lie, his mom loved jewelry and Patsy had an eye for finding beautiful stones, plus she had the creds to be able to get in. Perfect plan. If he could convince her, that is.

He decided to call Jamal to see how he was doing, Patsy had given him the house phone number. He didn't know people even had house phones these days, but maybe it was so he could call his family in Turkey. If it was over the internet, rather than a cell phone, that would make a lot of sense. VoIP was nearly free, just the internet cost.

He punched in the number and it rang a few times before Jamal answered with a weak hello.

"Hey buddy, this is Steve, I hear from Patsy, I mean Patricia, that you are sick. Anything I can do to help?"

"No, I'm just going to die here in peace. Are you staying with her? You do not want to come anywhere near this house. In fact, I think the national guard has put up a quarantine sign. Or if they haven't, they should."

Steve chuckled. "Yeah, I'm staying with her. I'm betting you'll feel good as new by Monday, maybe a few pounds lighter, but not dying either."

"From your mouth to God's ears. And now I am going back to bed, but thanks for letting me know you're good. I was worried Patricia might punch you in the nose."

"No, she fumed a little and muttered under her breath, but she let me come stay." Steve paused for a moment and then continued. "I hope to have the chance to work things out with her. So, while I wish you weren't sick, thanks."

"Sure, not my pleasure, but I'm glad you've found a silver lining for my pain and suffering."

"I did my friend. I hope I see you Sunday night or at least by Monday morning, when the real summit starts."

He heard Jamal sigh. "I hope so too, good luck with Patricia."

"Your mouth to God's ears."

CHAPTER 5

*P*atricia was almost finished with her last class of the day when the auditorium door opened, and Steve slipped into the back row. Her body went on alert, that man could always make her want him, just by showing up.

Dammit, what was he doing in her class, and what was she talking about before he'd walked in and killed her train of thought? She looked at her students, they were all busily writing. What had they been doing?

She casually walked over to the lectern and looked at her class outline and the time. Oh, right the mini description of the rock on the table, the specs of which were on the board. Good, nothing she needed to do then. They would finish and hand in their pages on their way out.

She scowled at Steve and he gave her a bright sunny smile, which warmed her insides, but made her even angrier at him. Bad man, she didn't want him warming her insides with his devastating smile. How could she hide from him tonight when he was sitting in her classroom?

Clearly, he still knew her too well. The problem was, trying to think of an excuse to get away from him wasn't working, there was nothing going on tonight. The women's basketball game was an away game. The men's team played tomorrow night. The baseball team had a bye this week. She didn't have tickets to the concert at Red Rocks. Darn it, there had to be something.

The bell rang and the students started filing out of the auditorium up the stairs, leaving their assignments on the table in the back of the room. None of them came up to ask her any questions, they all just walked out the door, leaving her with him. He got up as the last student left, collected the assignment papers from the table, and brought them down the stairs to her.

"So, did you think of an excuse to avoid me?"

"No, dammit, I didn't." She folded her arms across her chest.

"Excellent, then let's go have some dinner and talk."

"I don't really want to talk to you," she said sharply.

His smile was sad. "I know, but I think we need to, don't you? If nothing else for some closure."

She huffed and nodded. "Fine, I suppose it would make the next week easier if we got things off our chest. But I'm not sure I want to do that in public."

"Which is why I bought a rotisserie chicken and some potato salad, and have one in the oven and the other in the fridge at your house, along with a nice bottle of wine and some strawberry cheesecake."

"Well, I suppose if you're going to feed me, I can listen to what you have to say. Okay let's go get this over with. Did you walk or drive?"

"Walked, do you need to go by your office first?"

"No, not really." She took the papers from him and put them in her backpack. "I can just take these home."

As they walked up the hill to her house Patricia felt like

throwing up, not from the stomach flu Jamal had, but from the nervous tension. She did not want to have this conversation. She did not want to relive the past. She did not want to feel that pain again. Nope, if she had to rank it, this conversation would be dead last after a root canal and a pap smear and a mammogram—all on the same day.

They went in the house and she could smell the chicken, it probably would *normally* smell great, but right now it turned her stomach.

Steve asked, "Do you want to eat now?"

"No, but a big glass of wine might be good, or a shot of tequila."

He smiled. "It won't be that bad, but I did open some Pinot Noir before I walked down to campus, it should be ready to drink now. I'll pour you a glass while you get comfortable."

"I'll take you up on that, I need to go put my bag away and get out of my work clothes."

Patricia went to her bedroom and put her bag on the floor, she would deal with it later. She flopped down on her bed just needing a moment to chill, before she went to hear Steve's excuses for marrying someone else ten years ago. But it didn't help, her gut was churning and her mind was whirling. Might as well just go get it over with.

Now what to wear, her oldest rattiest sweats to turn him off? No, she had too much pride for that, jeans it was, but maybe not her sexiest jeans. Oh, hell, who was she kidding, she wanted to look awesome, and it would be a kind of armor. She put on some great jeans and a pretty shirt that made her eyes look more green than gray, and fluffed her hair.

Patricia found Steve in the living room looking out the window toward the mountains. One of the reasons she lived on a hill above campus was for the view of the Rockies.

Flopping down on the couch, she picked up a pillow to hold in her lap and grabbed her wine glass. "Okay, I'm ready, let's get this over with." She took a big gulp of wine as Steve settled in the chair next to the couch. He turned toward her, and she held her breath.

Steve put his elbows on his knees and held out his hands toward her. "I never meant to hurt you. At the time I thought what I was doing was—for the better good—I guess."

He shrugged. "You were on that expedition in Mexico for your summer project and research thesis. And I was seeing Katerina, more as friends than anything. We weren't sleeping together, just going out occasionally for dinner or a movie."

A co-worker? Likely story.

"I was an engineer and making good money, and Katerina was a student and interning at my company, between her junior and senior year in college. We hit it off when we were working on a project. So, when I invited her to have dinner with me one night, I paid for the meal. I didn't see it as a date, just co-workers eating together after a long day. I admit, I was missing you, and having someone to grab a bite to eat with, well, it just felt nice."

Her head was spinning, not dating? Then why the hell did he marry her?

He fidgeted and took another drink of wine, then continued, "So we were about two weeks from her internship being over, when Katerina's life fell apart. Her mother died unexpectedly from a heart attack. Katerina and her younger brother Thomas were living at home and going to school. Thomas was about to start his senior year of high school and her mom had been paying for college."

Steve rubbed his hands on his knees and continued with his story. "Katerina had assumed that her mom was paying for it from the life insurance from her father's death a few years earlier. But after her mother died, she realized that her mom had taken out a second mortgage on the house and was paying for Katerina's school out of that. She also found out that—although her mother made good money as a personal assistant—she was living paycheck to paycheck, and had very little life insurance. About enough to get her mother buried and that was all."

Patricia didn't like where this was going one bit. Steve had always had a soft heart and wanted to help people. That's part of the reason he was an environmental engineer, in order to help save the planet. Steve was a saver.

She heard her thoughts echoed in his next words. "So, when Katerina came to me and told me that she was losing the house, she would not be able to finish her education, and she didn't know what to do, I felt sorry for her. I told her I would be happy to help her out. When she said she couldn't possibly take help from her boyfriend, I was shocked that she thought about us that way. But as I continued to think about it, I realized I had acted like one, and I looked at her, so pretty, even with her tear streaked face. I felt affection for her and decided that maybe it was even love. I could help her. If we got married she and Thomas could live with me, they could both continue their education and Katerina and I could learn to love each other."

She was flabbergasted at his thought process. He'd said he was in love with her and they had planned to get married, dammit.

"My heart hurt at not having you as my wife, but you are a strong woman and self-sufficient and I knew some other lucky guy would snap you up—as soon as I was out of the picture."

She threw the pillow at him which he caught easily. "Dammit Steve, do you know what I was doing while you were being the self-sacrificing hero? I was working out how to change from the PhD program to the master's program, so I would only have one more year of school instead of three. I was planning to put aside my dream, because I missed you so damn bad."

She watched as all the blood drained from his face. "Oh Patsy, I'm so sorry. I had no idea, I mean I know we had talked about getting married and all that but… I don't know what to say, other than I'm sorry. So. Fucking. Sorry."

She crossed her arms and hardened her heart. "So, continue on, what happened with this match made in heaven?"

"Match made in hell, is more like it. So, I convinced her we should get married and they could move in with me. Their house was repossessed, and Katerina was held responsible for some of the debt her mother had accumulated. But with me supporting her, she went back to school and graduated and then stayed on for a graduate degree. Thomas joined the army as soon as he was out of high school. We slowly paid off all of her mother's debt."

He turned the pillow around in his hands, then set it down on the floor and rubbed his hand along his bearded chin, which made a rasping sound. "I couldn't prove it, but I thought Katerina was cheating on me. She denied it and told me some song and dance that it was just her working hard to advance in her new job. But since I was accusing her of such things, she needed some space, so she moved into the spare room."

The woman was using him, that bitch. She was obviously cheating on him, even if she'd only gotten a master's degree she wouldn't have been in her new job long enough to be trying to advance by working longer hours. How could he be so dense? She picked up the other pillow on the couch and drew it into her lap.

"The problem was, that by then I had realized, I didn't really love her and didn't give a crap if she was in the other room or not. Our sex life had been mediocre, so it wasn't a hardship, I figured someday we would have to deal with it, but I was working on a big project and I just didn't want to take the time out to force the issue. Color me surprised when she served me with divorce papers the day after I paid off the last of her mother's debt."

Patricia gasped. "She didn't."

"Oh yes, she did, she waited until the check cleared, called every creditor and made sure there was nothing left, and had her attorney serve me the papers. She'd written them up months prior and was just waiting until she was clear financially."

"What a bitch. Did you sue her for it in the divorce?" She shook her head and answered her own question. "No of course you didn't. God, Steve that really sucks."

"Yes, it did, we were married for six years and she managed to manipulate me the entire time. But I'm actually glad to be divorced, it was expensive, but it was an eye-opening experience. I'm not as soft hearted as I was, so who knows if the lesson learned will keep me from even bigger stupidities."

She saw the bitterness and humiliation in his face and her heart broke. "Having a soft and loving heart is not a bad thing, Steve. There are users in this world and you clearly hooked up with one. Don't let one bitch ruin your loving heart."

"Thanks, Patsy, but the worst part of this whole crap-tastic tale, is that I hurt you. I wish I could take it back, not for the financial reason, but because I lost you."

Yeah, he had lost her. He'd broken her heart ten years ago, and even though she felt sorry for him and realized it wasn't about her inadequacies, she was still not going back there. "Well, life goes on, and sometimes it sucks."

He gave her a sad smile, obviously reading between the lines accurately. "Well let's eat some chicken, shall we?"

CHAPTER 6

Steve woke early the next morning, still on east coast time. He got up, put on some jeans and went downstairs to make coffee. His talk with Patsy last night had gone well and they'd been able to chat comfortably during dinner. At least she didn't hate him anymore.

He didn't know if they would make it back to their former closeness, but at least they both had closure and could be friends. Not that he was happy to leave it like that, but it was a good place for now. And maybe he could convince her to go to the mountains and look for rocks today, maybe amethysts or whatever she thought would be best.

Steve tried to think of a way to broach the subject, as he measured out the coffee and put it on to brew. He looked in the fridge, to see what she had to whip up for breakfast. Maybe just some good old-fashioned scrambled eggs and bacon. She had cheese and some veggies he could scramble in with them. There were potatoes, so he could make some hash browns, breakfast was his favorite meal, so he could make about anything. He started chopping and shredding and frying bacon.

The coffee was finishing when Patsy stumbled into the kitchen. She was dressed in yoga pants and a huge t-shirt with the college mascot on it—that had seen better days—it was ragged and had a couple of stains on it. Her hair was messy, and she had no makeup on. But he was instantly drawn to her, he took one look at her and wanted to drag her back to bed and spend the next few hours—or days—worshipping every inch of her body.

Instead, he smiled. "Breakfast is about ready."

She frowned at him. "Why are you making a mess in my kitchen, Steve?"

"Cooking breakfast, it's the most important meal of the day."

"I smelled coffee and couldn't go back to sleep. I didn't want to wake up so early. Why are you up so early anyway?"

"Still on east coast time, and I want to get into the mountains today. I want to see if I can collect some stones for my mom and sisters while I'm here. Maybe from one of the mines. If I can still find one. It's been a few years; do you have time to show me where they are? If we go to the abandoned ones and get caught you could flash your geologist creds and keep us out of trouble."

She just stared at him and he could see her mind whirling trying to think of a way to get out of going with him. At least that's what he assumed she was thinking. But he'd caught her before she had coffee, so she wasn't thinking as quickly as normal.

"Please, my mom would love a stone that I found all on my own and you are the best at things like that. I had planned to ask Jamal to go with me but…" He turned the heat off under the eggs and buttered the last two pieces of toast.

She grimaced. "Poor guy. I suppose I can go with you, but I don't really want to be gone all day. With the summit starting tomorrow night I have things I need to get done." She took a drink of her coffee and he could see her thinking through the options. "So, we can't go over to Grand Junction or down to Creede. But I do have permission to take students to a couple of other claims, providing we don't take a lot of ore, enough for a pendant or two would be fine."

Score! "Sure, no problem, we can come back any time you say. Sit down and let's have breakfast, I'll even clean the kitchen while you get dressed."

As they ate he decided to ask her about some of her other gem collecting trips. "I noticed yesterday you were wearing turquoise jewelry, did you find that on one of your class field trips?"

She nodded. "Yes, we had a field trip in Leadville. That area isn't mined much anymore but I can take students in and we can bring out a small amount of ore for personal and educational purposes. Since the turquoise was discovered as a byproduct of the gold mining in that area it's a really good learning experience, especially to show the students the effects of the old mining processes."

"Yeah, I remember going there as a freshman or sophomore, it's part of the reason I changed my major to environmental engineering."

"Lots of evidence of the need for environmental impact studies around the state, that's for sure. With all the new laws people have to be very careful what they do. It's a good thing, I think."

"Which is one of the reasons you're on the summit committee, I assume," he said.

"Yep. Ok you clean up while I go shower." She popped the last piece of bacon in her mouth and got up to go.

Then she stopped and looked at him. "The best place for

rock hounding is probably Mt. Antero by Buena Vista, it's close enough for a day trip. The problem is that it's so high up that they don't normally open the roads for a few more weeks. But we've had such a dry winter, they might be open early to try to make up for the crappy ski season we had this year, maybe get some tourists in for spring break. There are some nice aquamarines there as well as topaz and smoky quartz."

Patsy stopped speaking and looked out the window for a moment before continuing. "Do you want to call the highway department and see if it's accessible? If it's not, Ruby Mountain should be open, it's mostly garnets and yellow topaz, but I've seen some pretty stones from there."

"You got it. Do you want me to make some sandwiches or something to take with us, you seem to have a fridge full of food? I could make us a picnic."

"That's a good idea, there's an insulated pack in the mud room. The highway department number is on the fridge next to my teaching schedule that you obviously already found. You can call and make food while I get dressed. You're kind of handy to have around," she said as she walked out of the room.

Steve smiled as she left. He was spending the day with Patsy doing something she loved. Excellent progress.

PATRICIA SMILED ON THE WAY TO HER ROOM AND THEN stopped short. Wait a minute, she had just agreed to spend the day with Steve. Did she really want to do that, or did she get caught up in the moment? She shrugged and continued on, anytime someone talked about going rock hunting she got excited. It was the main reason she was a geologist, she loved nothing more than being outside in the fresh air looking at rocks.

How did the saying go, she'd go with the trash hauler, yeah that was it and it actually fit her pretty well. But she'd seen the trash hauler, he was an older guy with just a few strings of hair in a comb-over and dirty ragged overalls. He was a scavenger, she'd seen him digging through trash bags looking for treasure, so he would probably jump at the chance. But she'd rather take Steve, any day. And he'd been through some of the same geology classes, so he had a basic understanding of rock hounding, and he knew she loved it, the sneaky guy.

She'd been excited about rocks since she was a kid. Growing up they'd had a gravel driveway filled with rocks. Most of them just ordinary gray gravel but occasionally she would find a really pretty stone hidden among the others. And when her family had gone camping in the mountains, she'd been in hog heaven, or maybe rock heaven.

Patricia's older sister had spent most of the time in the tent doing sewing crafts or reading. Her brother would spend the day at the lake or river fishing with their dad. But she had spent the days looking at the ground, finding rocks, reveling in the discovery of something she had never seen before, and wondering why rocks were different in each new location.

Her parents had bought her books on rocks, since she'd had many more questions, than they'd had answers for. They always encouraged her curiosity and didn't even blink, when she had said she wanted to go to the mineral engineering school in the foothills of Colorado, to study geology. It was not a traditional choice for a woman, but that didn't faze them in the least, they had always encouraged each of their children to believe they were free, and intelligent enough to do whatever they put their mind to. She was allowed to follow her curiosity and her own choices.

She'd met so many other people who had parents not so supporting, those friends doubted every single choice they made and their own abilities. It had taken her a long time to realize what a blessing her parents had been in her formative years, to encourage each of their children to follow their interests and dreams. They had never compared them with their siblings, freeing them to follow their God-given nature.

When she got out of the shower Patricia put on heavy jeans and hiking boots, on top she wore a tank top and then a long-sleeved shirt over it, and grabbed a sweatshirt to go over that, she had a raincoat, parka, gloves and a hat in the Rav4.

You could never tell what the weather would be like, and it could change on a dime. So, layers were a requirement. She put her hair in a ponytail and grabbed the sunscreen and lip balm. Her backpack of geological necessities was also in the car, folding shovel, rock hammer, hand lens, binoculars, compass, field notebook and colored pencils. Along with all the emergency equipment she always carried with her. She could probably camp out in her car for a week and not run out of the essentials.

Patricia walked into the kitchen to see Steve adding some cookies to the top of the backpack of food. "Look at you, all ready to go."

She looked him over and decided he hadn't gotten soft, and still remembered about Colorado weather, he was dressed in layers too. But somehow, he still looked sexy even dressed in hiking clothes. His well-worn jeans fit him perfectly and his long-sleeved shirt had the sleeves rolled up to his elbows, exposing strong, tanned arms with a sprinkling of dark hair. He had a hoodie and jacket on the counter, next to the backpack filled with food and water. He looked good enough to eat, but she was—by God—not going there.

"Well let's head out. I also thought about Red Feather Lake. I take the students there and they always find some amethysts. What did the highway department have to say? Red Feather is north and Mt. Antero and Ruby Mountain are south, so we need to make a decision."

"They didn't mention Mt. Antero as being closed on the recording, so I assume that means it's open. I vote south because there are two possibilities. We should probably take your car; I didn't get an SUV. That's a pretty little Rav4 you've got out in the driveway."

"Yeah, I just got it a few months ago, my old beater finally gave up the ghost. So, when I went into the dealership, I told them I had two requirements, that it had hands free calling and that it was blue, I was sick of the gun-metal gray. I looked at Honda's too but the only colors they had were black, white, gray, and red, they could order me a navy blue one, but it would take six weeks. I didn't really want navy, so when I looked at the Rav and it came in that bright blue. I was sold. I'd heard a lot of good reports on the model."

Steve laughed at her story. "Sounds just like you, practical first, researching the makes and models and then whimsical at the end with the bright blue."

"Yep all me, plus my vehicle is already loaded with all the gear we could possibly need. We could stop at the hot springs on the way back, did you bring a pair of swim trunks with you?"

"No, it never occurred to me I would need swim trunks in April in Colorado."

She laughed. "True, if we do decide to stop, they probably have some you could purchase. Let's get moving, if we go up to the summit of Mt. Antero it takes a while, the road is rough and slow going."

"I'm ready now." Steve shouldered the lunch pack and grabbed his jackets. She led the way outside.

Patricia was pleasantly surprised when he walked over to the passenger's side and got in after stowing the lunch pack and jackets in the rear seat. A lot of men insisted they had to be the ones to drive, even if it wasn't their own vehicle. She was glad to see he hadn't turned into one of those guys.

They got moving toward their destination, it would take a couple hours to get to Nathrop, before they started the climb up the mountain which was another forty-five minutes at least, on dirt roads.

She had no idea what to talk to him about for that long. They had talked about their careers and the summit during lunch yesterday and then talked through his reasons for dumping her last night. Maybe his family would be a safe subject or hers. The radio was on and that filled in some background noise, but as they got on the highway heading north the silence started getting to be too much.

She said, "So how is your family?"

At the same time, he asked, "Where is your sister living?"

They laughed and the tension broke. She answered him, "My sister is living in Hawaii, she's married and has two little kids, Brandon is six and Brooke is four. They are adorable and I try to go see them a couple of times a year, and we face-time every week or two. I want the kids to know me."

"Hawaii, huh? What island is she on? What's she doing there?"

"She's on the Big Island, we went there on vacation about eight years ago and went on a tour of one of the coffee farms, she hit it off with the tour guide, who was also the owner's son. It was a slow season and their normal tour guide had not shown up for work, so the son was filling in for the pre-booked tours. It was pretty much love at first sight—for both of them—so she spent some evenings with him while we were on vacation, and then they had an online relationship.

He came out here to visit during his vacation and they eventually got married. He had to help run the family farm, so she moved there. She's very happy. She's working at one of the resorts in the event planning arena. I asked her a lot of questions when I started helping with the energy summit."

"Good for her. What's your brother doing?"

She laughed, "Having kids, it seems like, he's got three boys and his wife is pregnant again. I need to buy him a TV, I think. But he keeps active and we all go jeeping every weekend or two from late spring to early fall. They seem to carefully time the pregnancies, so she's not very far along during that time of year, that way she doesn't have to miss anything. She's quite the adventurer. Most of the time it's her initiating the weekends and he just smiles and goes along with her."

Steve nodded. "Seems like he was always ready for whatever adventure came along. Are your parents still alive?"

She shook her head. "No, Dad died right after I got my master's degree, from a damn test they ran on him at the hospital, he was allergic to the dye and he'd been too sick to fight the reaction. It was just stupid, now all of us are terrified to have any kind of test that requires dye. In case we're allergic too. Mom just passed last summer, she had a liver problem and didn't know it, because she refused to go to the doctor after Dad died. By the time she started feeling bad and went to have it checked, it was too late."

"Oh, Patsy, that's awful, I'm so sorry."

"Yeah, it sucks." Her heart ached from missing them so damn bad. She had to change the subject it was too painful to think about it even now. She missed her dad just as much as she missed her mom, even though he'd been gone longer. After every milestone, she still found herself thinking she should call them and let them know. She'd even picked up the phone to call several times, before realizing there was no one to call.

She swallowed to get the knot in her throat to go down. "How is your family?"

"Doing quite well, Mom and Dad are currently on a cruise, he sold his business about a year ago, and has finally let go of *teaching* the new owners about it, enough that Mom convinced him to go on a cruise. She's always wanted to, and he would never go because he couldn't leave the business long enough. My sisters are both good too. One's married and has a son, her husband is in the army and is deployed a lot. The other is busy with her career and says she doesn't have time for men."

"Let me guess. Theresa is married, and Rebecca is busy with her career."

Steve laughed out loud. "Right on the button, pretty clever of you."

"Not too much, Rebecca was always more career oriented, taking jobs to further her education and Theresa was always babysitting some neighbors kid."

"I never thought of it that way, but you're right."

"So, do you have any kids?"

Steve didn't say anything for a very long time, then he sighed. "No, Katerina didn't want any and she made sure she didn't get pregnant. Except one time, shortly before she divorced me, she got pregnant. She didn't tell me, until after she had aborted it. I was devastated, I always wanted kids. I just shut down. I couldn't talk about it and I couldn't just let it go. I withdrew, so it wasn't as much of a surprise when she had me served divorce papers, and I came home to find she had moved out."

Patricia had to fight to keep tears from forming in her eyes, she was on a highway, she had to be able to see to drive. There was a huge lump in her throat. She finally swallowed it away. "I don't know what to say, Steve, except I'm sorry for your loss."

He cleared his throat. "Thanks, but maybe we should talk about something else. How about them Broncos?"

She laughed, it was a familiar way to change the subject. Nearly everyone from Colorado was a Bronco fan, so there was always an opinion on them.

CHAPTER 7

HELLUVA
ENGINEER

hey kept the discussion light as they finished their drive to Buena Vista, chatting about the scenery they were passing and some of their interests. But Patricia kept thinking about what he had revealed, she was softening toward him and she knew that was a bad idea. He'd broken her heart—out of good intentions it seemed—and he'd gotten his heart broken in return. He had always talked about having a family, they had both wanted children.

She could not imagine how he had felt when he found out about the abortion, and then been served with divorce papers. She wanted to go smack his ex-wife, and at the same time she wanted to smack him for being a dumbass and marrying her in the first place. At least she had the satisfaction of knowing she would have been a better wife. Didn't change anything, but it was something.

They passed a lot of little towns, and at the last one before they hit the Mt. Antero road she stopped for a potty break. Once she turned off the highway and onto the summit drive it would be unpopulated.

"Pit stop time, no bathrooms on the summit and we might as well fill up the tank."

He nodded. "Sounds good. I'll pump the gas; you go on in."

"You don't need to it's my car." She protested.

"But it's my trip and we ate your food this morning. I'll pay for the gas."

"Okay, you win, here are the keys, you don't need to use them, just keep them in your pocket, it's got keyless entry." She handed him the keys and stepped out of the car, stretching her muscles after the drive. Once she'd used the facilities, she spent some time wandering around the little store giving Steve time. He had the keys and she enjoyed these mom and pop stores. One could never tell what might be found.

They had all the typical things, postcards, mini license plates with names on them, native American jewelry, hand-made saltwater taffy, and jars of jam. They also had some unique items and homemade crafts that might appeal to tourists that emphasized all things Colorado. Columbines and aspen leaves in all forms from jewelry to wall hangings to knickknacks. Beads from the different ores found in the mountains, small vials of gold and silver flakes, and the ever-popular buffalo jerky.

"See anything you desperately need?"

She turned to look at Steve grinning at her. "Nope just checking out the creativity of people. Ready to roll?"

"Yep, the tank is full, and I got some buffalo jerky." He held up the tiny pouch that probably cost him a pretty penny.

She shook her head at him, and they went out to get back on the road. A few minutes later she turned off the highway and onto the Mt. Antero road that would get them to the summit. It did appear to be open, so they started up the rough road, it was gravel and had a ton of switchbacks.

They didn't talk much as she drove carefully up the road. She needed her concentration for navigation, and Steve knew it. He didn't seem nervous about her driving though, which was a relief, nervous passengers only made the driver more nervous, and she didn't need that on a difficult road.

The dirt road ended, and she continued along a jeep trail until she could go no further and parked her car. "We'll have to hike the rest of the way. Doesn't look like we'll need the coats, but better bring them anyway, you never know in the mountains, a perfectly clear day can change in an instant."

She remembered one time when hiking with her girl scout troop and a beautiful summer day had turned into a thunder and lightning storm that had them scurrying to get off the mountain and down below timberline, so they weren't the tallest things on the mountain. The sky had turned black with clouds that had killed their visibility and the rain caused the path to turn into slick mud. It was something she'd never forgotten, getting soaking wet, and being terrified.

She got out of the car and stretched her back and legs, to get them warmed up and ready for the hike. Sunscreen and lip balm were a requirement, it was a clear sunny day and at this altitude they would burn easily, and the high dry mountain air would chap their lips if they didn't take precautions. Steve came around to the back with his pack and hoodie on, his coat tied on the pack, she threw him the sunscreen and he smiled his thanks and applied it to his face and hands. She held up the lip balm, but he shook his head and patted his pocket to indicate he had his own.

She put the sunscreen and lip balm in the pack, slid her arms through the straps and they started out. They fell into step with each other and it seemed like the years fell away, and they were back where they had been ten years ago.

Hiking into the mountains to go exploring, she had many fond memories of their time spent in the wilderness. A lot of weekends they had escaped the shenanigans happening at school and had gone off together for their own fun.

They had spent a lot of those weekends having sex, but it had also been the companionship that had lured them off campus. She had missed those weekends—with him more than anything else—when he graduated and moved back east.

STEVE NOTICED PATSY HAD GOTTEN QUIET AS THEY STARTED off. He wondered if she was remembering other weekend trips they had taken to go exploring the mountains and plains of Colorado. They had both enjoyed the solitude and beauty they found on their excursions.

Patsy interrupted his thoughts. "You know I have an idea, so many people have been up here digging and staking claims in the last few years, but I've always wondered about a slightly different area. Are you game for trying it? It might yield nothing, there might be a very good reason why no one digs in that area, but you never know. According to my calculations of the beds and how they are laid down, I see an equal likelihood that there could be something there. What do you think?"

Since he was less interested in actually finding stones—than he was in simply spending time with Patsy—he was more than willing to go off on a tangent with her. If they found nothing, but spent the day together, he would have accomplished his goal. If they did find something, especially on her educated hunch, she would be thrilled.

He looked over at her and nonchalantly shrugged. "Sure, why not, you probably know as much about the possibilities as all these other people. Let's go for it."

She beamed at him and took off in a new direction. The direction she took didn't have any paths like the way they had been heading. Up here above timberline the undergrowth did not grow back easily, so the paths most people took were clear.

As if she had read his mind, she turned toward him. "Try to stay on rock as much as possible so we don't damage the plants."

"I was just thinking that very thing." They continued in the direction she had chosen, but took it a little slower to pick their way along, staying on rock or dirt as much as possible and when they had to, walking softly on the grass and brush that managed to live at this altitude.

He noticed her continuing to look at outcroppings and occasionally taking a pocketknife and scraping away dirt to see what kind of rock was underneath. After she discovered what it was, she would put the dirt back and press it into place. She eventually stopped and he watched as she checked her compass and used some tools to look at the slope of the land and the distance to the peak. She bent down and scraped away dirt, then she went over to the outcropping and scraped away some of the surface of it.

She smiled and dropped down and carefully scraped away more dirt at the foot of the outcropping. She looked up at him and took off her pack. "Let's try here."

He went over and put his pack next to hers, she pulled out a little folding shovel, her rock hammer, and another small hand shovel that looked kind of like a garden trowel with sharp edges.

She took her folding shovel and snapped it into place,

51

handing it to him to start digging. He would dig a little and then she would look through what he dug up. He was down maybe a foot when he felt his shovel hit a harder stone.

"I just hit something not as soft as the other has been."

"Too solid for the shovel?"

He pushed in more. "Yeah, it is."

She handed him her rock hammer. "Give it a couple of whacks with this and see what happens. Not too hard, but not too soft either. Safety goggles first, though." She gave him a pair and she put on a second pair.

Steve took the rock hammer and aimed the point toward the rock and hit it, nothing moved. He felt her watching over his left shoulder. He hit it two more times and the rock cracked and kind of caved in. "Oh, it caved in."

"Wait, don't hit it again." Patsy took out a small chisel and wedged it in the crack. She moved it back and forth. Then she moved the chisel to another area and did the same thing, until she had worked around in kind of a circle but based on the places the rock had cracked. When she got back to where she started a piece came loose, Patsy pulled it out and held it up, there were some clear crystals on one side.

She handed it to him and got her hand lens out of her pack. Patsy looked closely at it and then beamed up at him. "It looks like Beryl alright, which is the base stone for aquamarine, the tint of the stone makes it aquamarine, not the composition. Let's see if we can get a bit more out."

He made his hole wider until more of the harder rock was exposed and then used the rock hammer to break through. They pulled up a few more pieces that also had crystals on them, but these had a slight tint. They continued to pull crystals out and the color got more pronounced, a little more blue or gray.

Patsy stopped working. "I'm going to grab the water

bottles; we can't get dehydrated up here."

"Good idea, I've got one piece that's almost loose and then I'll join you." His stomach rumbled. "We should probably have some lunch too."

She grinned at him. "I'll get it all out then."

He finally pulled out the piece he was working on and it had several crystals that were the light blue color of aquamarine. "He jumped up and took it over to her. Look, is this it?"

She grinned. "Yes, at least it sure looks like it to me, we did it."

He grabbed her around the waist and swung her around in pure joy, as she laughed.

PATRICIA WAS SO EXCITED; IT WAS HER FIRST MAJOR FIND AND it wasn't where everyone else always looked. Her expertise had suggested they look in this direction and she rejoiced in what they had found. As Steve swung her around, she reveled in the accomplishment of it, and wondered if they should stake a claim. It might be a good idea.

Steve finally put her back on her feet and they held on to each other, both a bit dizzy from the elation. She was laughing up at him in pure exhilaration. Then the atmosphere changed, and they sobered. He looked in her eyes and then down at her mouth. He looked back in her eyes and she could see desire building in them.

Oh no, not kissing, this was not a good idea, she needed to stop it immediately. But she stayed in his arms and just couldn't move. He looked in her eyes and then started to lower his head. She wanted to move away or say something snarky that would break the spell, but she couldn't. She couldn't move, she couldn't speak, she could barely breathe.

Steve lowered his head slowly, giving her plenty of time to pull away or push him back, but she couldn't, she was trapped. His mouth brushed hers in a kiss so soft, so tentative, she almost couldn't feel it. But her lips tingled, her blood raced, and she sighed. She needed more, so she raised up on her toes to meet him more fully. Patricia pressed her lips to his, firmer than that first light touch and he hauled her body into his. He deepened the kiss, she opened to him and he swept inside.

Hunger pounded through her and she grabbed his hair with both hands and pulled his head down, not letting him go. He wrapped his arms around her and groaned. When they couldn't go any longer without breath, they pulled back and stared into each other's eyes. She saw hunger and lust and yearning, reflected back at her and she hoped she didn't look as vulnerable to him as he did to her.

Patricia wanted more, she wanted him with everything she had, she wanted to strip him naked and have her merry way with him right here in the broad daylight. She couldn't handle more, so she pushed away from him and turned toward the lunch. She laughed shakily. "Let's eat."

"Patsy…"

"Just eat, Steve, and pretend that never happened." She couldn't talk about it, not now, maybe never. Long buried feelings had rushed forth and nearly overwhelmed her with yearning. She burned for him, she wanted him, she craved him. She stuffed those emotions down. Not going there.

"But…"

"No, I insist, that was just the joy of discovery pouring out, nothing more. Now eat." Patricia doubted she convinced him, but she was darn sure she was going to convince herself. It was just the thrill of the moment. With shaking hands, she picked up a sandwich.

CHAPTER 8

*A*s they ate, she kept the conversation focused on their discovery. Patsy talked about the various colors Beryl could take and how the different colorings made the same basic rock into different gems. He didn't need a geology lesson, but he assumed her blabbering on about it kept her from thinking about that kiss.

They finished eating and packed up the food. There was another hour or two left where they could stay and work, before they needed to start down the mountain. The road was too treacherous to drive in the dark, they needed to be off before night hit. The switchbacks were too severe.

Steve worked next to Patsy as they pulled a few more crystals from the ground. He didn't know exactly what to say to her. She had obviously enjoyed his kisses but then she'd pulled back behind a wall that kept him out. Those kisses had made him feel whole again, something he hadn't felt in years.

After a long silence where he thought about the whole episode, he finally decided to go back to discussing their tiny mine. "So, are you going to stake a claim on our find?"

"I've been thinking about that; I've never done something

like it before. It would be nice to have my very own area I could bring students to. I could explain to them how I extrapolated where the bed should run and how I, um we, made the discovery." She smiled at him. "It might make a good paper, too. You know us academic types always need to be writing papers."

"Yeah and it's not necessary to bring me into it, I did nothing but follow your lead." He shrugged. "And some digging."

"Which was quite welcome, having my own personal excavator is always a pleasure."

"It's my great honor to wield a shovel at your command," he said laughing and taking a bow. When he looked back at her he could literally see the walls go up, before she bent down to continue picking at the rocks. He'd done that to her —he supposed—made her so leery of him. She'd never been that way in the past she was always open and loving. He wondered if she was closed off to all men or just him.

More importantly, he wondered if there was anything he could do to repair the damage he'd done to her. He would have to think about that, he didn't have a lot of time before he would be headed back east to his family, friends, and job. But maybe there was something he could do. Some way to teach her that he and other people were dependable and wouldn't go around hurting her.

He wished he could turn back time and redo some things in his life, with the knowledge he had now. Because he was pretty certain if he did go back with only the knowledge he had then, he would do the same damn thing over again.

He'd been so certain he was taking the best action by helping Katerina and her brother. Couldn't forget about her brother, he had been nearly as lost and confused as Katerina. Thomas was several years younger and just finishing up high school. He'd gone straight into the Army, so hadn't been around to watch the shit show their life became when Katerina no longer needed him.

He was glad Thomas had been spared the ugliness, because they still had a good relationship. Not real close, since Thomas was based out of Louisiana and been deployed a lot, but they emailed, Facebooked, and Instagramed back and forth, and sometimes even facetimed. That didn't happen too often, especially when Thomas was not in the country.

He hadn't heard from Thomas in a while, but he was deployed so that wasn't uncommon. He should send him some books and a care package. He hadn't done that in a while.

PATSY WONDERED WHAT STEVE WAS THINKING ABOUT. HE'D gotten really quiet. She hadn't meant to shut him down when he was joking about being under her command. She'd just felt such a yearning for him to be by her side. It was silly really, she knew he was only here for the week and then would be going back to Virginia, where he worked, and his family lived.

They had always planned to live near his family, they were so close. Her family was close too, but not in a live in each other's pocket kind of way. They were happy to travel around to see each other a couple of times a year.

But that was then, and this was now. So, he would be going back to Virginia and she would stay here. They had a few days to be together and then that would be that. She would go back to dating occasionally and teaching her students. She had a good life and she wasn't going to get involved with Steve again, so it wouldn't break her heart a second time when he left, and that was all there was to it.

She straightened and looked at the time. "We should probably head out; it's going to take us a while to get back to the Rav and then down the mountain. I'm surprised we had such good weather today, it's so early in the season for it."

He stood up and smiled. "I'm ready, we have quite a few rocks to take with us."

"Yeah, we'll clean them up and then you can take your pick." She got her flashlight out and shined it into the hole they had dug. "There's a lot more in there, it looks like. It would be a fun place to bring students." She took down the coordinates, it was amazing the apps they had for phones these days.

"Should we put the dirt back into the hole? So, no one finds it?"

"Good question, I'm not really worried about people finding it and stealing it, but I don't want the dirt we dug out to wash down the mountain and cause problems either. So maybe we should put it back in."

They started carefully putting the dirt and rocks back into the hole they had dug. When she came back it would be easy for her to bring it back out to show her students. Plus, it would be good for the kids to do some digging to get to the formation.

When they were finished, she patted it down and he gathered a few large loose rocks to put on top of it to keep it from washing away in the rain. Then they gathered up their gear and headed toward the road. It always seemed farther walking back than it did the coming out, but they finally got to her vehicle and stored everything in the hatch.

They grabbed some water bottles out of the back to drink on the way back down. They could stop at the first town for a break and dinner before they drove back to campus. She glanced at him. "Do you want to stop at the hot springs?"

He shrugged. "I don't have a burning desire, but if you want to, I'm game."

"I think grabbing some dinner and heading back would be a better idea, with the summit starting tomorrow night, it would probably be wise to make this an early evening. Those reception things can last forever."

"Sounds like a good idea. Although I would not have been opposed to seeing you in a sexy swimsuit."

She felt her cheeks heat, but kept her eyes on the road. "Just a simple one piece, nothing sexy."

He didn't answer and she wondered what he was thinking. As they got closer to town, she questioned if she had been too hasty about not going to the hot springs, it would give them something to do, rather than sit at her house all night. They would have several hours before she could claim fatigue and go to bed. What would they do?

Yeah, maybe the hot springs wasn't such a bad idea after all. If they did that for an hour and then had dinner and drove back. Unloaded the stuff and maybe they could clean up the rocks some. All that would put it closer to bed time, when she could get away from him. Plus, the hot springs would help with any muscle soreness from all that digging.

Patricia cleared her throat. "So, I was thinking maybe the hot springs would be a good idea after all. It would help with any muscle fatigue from digging and hiking."

"Are you saying I'm out of shape and can't handle a little digging?"

She felt her face get hot, now he thought she was judging him. "Um, no, nothing like that I just thought…"

He laughed. "I'm just teasing you, I think the hot springs would be fun, let's do it."

Patricia breathed out a sigh of relief. "I thought we could go for an hour and then have some dinner before we head back, unless you're hungry now."

"And now you're saying I'm a pig, and cannot wait to have dinner?"

This time she glanced at him, saw the twinkle in his eyes, and slugged him in the arm. "Stop that."

He whimpered. "Ow, that hurt, you're too strong to hit poor defenseless guys like me."

She glanced at him again, at his pouty expression and laughed out loud. He couldn't hold it for long and laughed too.

"Well, aren't you just full of it tonight."

He just smiled and said nothing.

CHAPTER 9

Steve was having a great time, the best day he'd had
in, well, years. He couldn't remember the last time
he'd felt so happy. Patsy wasn't cold to him any longer, he
hadn't breached all her defenses—by any stretch of the imagination—but he'd gotten past maybe the shield and walls and
even the barbed wire. He still had a long way to go, but he
was a hell of a lot closer.

He didn't know why she had changed her mind about
going to the hot springs, but he was thrilled with the idea,
he'd been trying to think of how to keep her engaged with
him when they got back to her house. Figuring she would run
off to her room or office and lock him out.

Now, he got to spend more time with her. And although
he had been teasing her about a sexy swimsuit, he couldn't
deny the appeal of seeing her in a lot less clothes. He didn't
care whether it was one piece or a string bikini, one thin layer
of spandex would show off her curves and leave very little to
the imagination.

When they got into the little town of Nathrop she turned
into the resort. "I'm sure they have a store you can buy trunks

61

in. I can't imagine you're the only person to visit Colorado in the spring and not know to bring a swimsuit."

"Yeah, Colorado is not somewhere that you think of swimsuits when you're packing to visit. Most people think of snow and cold, maybe hiking and jeans type activities, but not swimsuits."

Once they had paid the day pass fee, and he'd bought a suit, they found the changing rooms, and then met outside. He about swallowed his tongue when he saw her, yes, her suit was one piece and she had a towel wrapped around the waist, but she looked amazing. The suit was lowcut in the front and was a bright turquoise color that drew his attention to her creamy skin.

That soft skin called him to worship it, with his hands and mouth, to touch and kiss and lick every square inch. His mind took him back to a time where he had done just that, and his body reacted. He was glad he had his towel around his waist as he dragged his mind back to the present and commanded his body to obey.

Patsy glanced at his chest for a minute, he thought he saw desire flare in her eyes, but it was gone so quickly he decided he must have imagined it, she cleared her throat. "I was thinking the pools would be the best bet. We could try the creekside area but it's a toss-up this time of year whether they will be hot, warm, or even a little cool, depending on the mountain runoff. Since we've had a really dry winter, they would probably be warm, but…"

"The pools are perfect. I don't want to be stumbling around in a creek when the sun is going down anyway."

She grinned at him. "Yeah, falling on the rocks right before the conference probably wouldn't be a great idea. We don't want to send Jamal into a heart attack, on top of his flu, poor guy."

"You don't think he would appreciate his keynote speaker or his right-hand woman on crutches?"

"No, not at all, he's got enough on his plate with the flu."

They started walking toward the pools. Steve said, "Yeah, I hope he's feeling better tomorrow, we should probably call and check on him in the morning, in case he's not going to make it to the reception. Is there anything we would need to do if he's not up to it?"

She tapped her finger on her lips, which zeroed his attention to them. He wanted to taste them again, and drink her in. She shook her head. "Nope, I can't really think of anything; we've had everything set up and finalized forever."

He just nodded dumbly because he had no idea what she was talking about, all he could think about were those lips he wanted to kiss and lick and consume.

He followed behind her as they got to the pool and she went over to one of the deck chairs, dropped her towel on it, and he nearly had a heart attack. Her suit was high cut on her hips and showed off her long, gorgeous legs. As she toed off her shoes all he could do was stare, burning up with desire for the woman who had no idea how close she was to being jumped. She looked back at him. "Last one in, is a rotten egg."

"That will be me because I have to get my shoes off. I'll meet you in there." He said lamely, he needed a moment to control himself before he took off the towel. He sat down on the other deck chair and made a big show of untying his shoes, which he totally didn't need to do, but he needed to buy some time to get composed.

Steve didn't think he should go around sporting a raging hard-on for everyone to see, it was a family place. Not that many people were around, but still. Then he heard her moan as she entered the water, and that just made things worse. Dear God, she was going to kill him.

PATRICIA COULDN'T FIGURE OUT WHY IT WAS TAKING STEVE so long to take off his shoes. She needed him to get in the damn pool, so she would stop staring at his bare chest. The man was built, and she wanted to touch, no lick, no bite him all over.

Her fingers itched to touch his washboard abs and she wanted to lick each muscle. He'd been fit and sexy ten years ago, but he had definitely improved with age and she wanted to feel and taste that improvement. If he would just get in the pool, she wouldn't be able to see as well and maybe she could calm down.

She should just turn her back, and look at the sunset, yeah, the sunset, very pretty. It wouldn't last long this high up in the mountains, so she should enjoy it while she could. But the hot guy behind her was a whole lot prettier, than the view of the mountains with the sun outlining them in bright colors. She was determined to resist the lure, so she stared at the sunset, not really seeing it, thinking about the sexy man at her back.

"It's beautiful up here isn't it." He startled her when he spoke, he'd snuck up on her while she was pretending to enjoy the view.

"Yes, it is. The hot water feels good too, don't you think."

"Yeah, I think my muscles are going to be glad for the soak."

"I thought your big, strong, macho self didn't need no hot springs."

He laughed. "Need, no. Appreciate, yes. I'm not stupid."

She smiled back at him and groaned inwardly, how could he look even better, up close and all wet. She turned back toward the sunset, but it was over, the sky turning dark.

Night fell quickly in the mountains.

The pools had lights, so it wasn't dark where they were. Dark might have been a better idea. The bright lights of the pool showed him too perfectly.

Maybe she could float in the water and close her eyes and then she wouldn't have to look at Mr. Hottie. Great idea, it would get her hair wet, but better than letting herself attack the man. She laid back in the water and heard Steve groan.

She kicked her feet to raise back up and asked, "Are you okay, I heard you groan did you pull a muscle or something?"

"No," he said sounding pissed.

"Then what's the problem, why do you sound ticked off? It can't be my concern for you, is it? I just thought you were joking about that."

"I was. It's nothing." He turned from her and started to swim away.

"Steve, tell me what's wrong."

He stopped swimming and stood. "Patsy stop, nothing's wrong," he said not looking at her.

"Bullshit, what is it?"

"Dammit, fine, you asked for it. It's you in that hot turquoise swimsuit looking like… I don't know… a forbidden treat I can't have. You're so damn beautiful and I just…"

She felt her face heat, way hotter than the water in the pool. "Oh, well, um, yeah. Time to swim." Then it was her turn to swim away.

She heard him chuckle. "You asked."

Yeah, she did, and she wasn't going to talk about it. So, he was feeling the lust thing too, well good to know she wasn't the only one. They did have a pretty intense history, but she didn't want to go back and revisit that. One broken heart per lifetime was her quota.

As she slowly swam down the length of the pool she wondered if maybe a little fling would help cool them both down. Kind of a no strings, get it out of the system, type of thing.

Could she do that? She had tried to have relationships with a few men in the last ten years, but whenever it had gotten to the point where they should be close enough to have sex, she'd backed off. When she couldn't handle the thought of having sex with them, she realized she didn't care for them enough to continue dating. Some of the guys hadn't been very happy with her, but she just couldn't handle sex with them.

And now here she was, contemplating a no strings sexual relationship with Steve, her one and only. Could she do that with him? Probably not a good idea, better steer clear of that whole thought.

She did a slow lazy lap of the pool; it wouldn't be good to do anything strenuous in the one-hundred-degree heat. But slow moving was good. When she got back to the other end she sat on the benches on the side of the pool and watched Steve moving toward her. Muscles bunching with each stroke of his arms, oh man, he looked so good. He was going to be living in her home for another seven days. She wasn't sure she wouldn't self-combust in that time.

He joined her on the built-in bench. "Sorry, didn't mean to make you uncomfortable."

"I know and if I'd let you swim off you wouldn't have, you were trying to be a gentleman and I didn't let you."

He shrugged. "I should have come up with some other excuse."

"I probably wouldn't have believed it and kept pestering you. So, it's my bad."

He just smiled at her.

She whispered, "I know how you were feeling."

He heard her even though she half hoped he couldn't. "We're bound to have some feelings like that in view of our past. But we're adults and can resist temptation."

"I'm not sure I want to… resist." She was inflamed with desire for this man, ten years was a damn long time, she wanted to feel the weight of his body, she wanted to feel him fill her, she wanted to have a glorious orgasm with the only man who made her burn.

"Patsy…"

"Well, we *are* adults, so we could just get it out of our system, a fling, no harm, no foul, no strings, no expectations. Just some stress relief." She didn't know if she was trying to convince him or herself. Yes, stress relief, but it would be more than that.

"I'm not sure that would work." Steve said.

"Well, if you're not interested…"

"I didn't say *that*."

"This *is* a hotel, we could just get a room tonight, have a little stress relief and drive back in the morning." Now she was nearly begging him, the more she thought about it, the more she wanted it, maybe even needed it.

He ran his hands through his hair and gripped it tight, pulling it. "Woman, you better make sure you know what you're suggesting."

She looked at him, he was gorgeous, and he was only here a week, how much trouble could happen to her heart in a week? Some yes, but would it be worth it, that was the real question.

They both sat there looking at each other in silence, thinking, assessing. She could see the thoughts running through his mind reflected in his eyes. Finally, she nodded, and he let out a breath he had apparently been holding.

"As long as you're sure," he said.

She wasn't sure at all, but she couldn't help herself. Patricia nodded again. "I'm sure."

He took her hand in his, and they slowly walked to the stairs and out of the pool. In silence, they wrapped their towels around themselves, slipped their shoes back on and started toward the locker rooms.

She said, "No sense getting dressed in our dusty clothes. "I'm just going to grab mine and get my bag out of the car, you get us a room while I do that."

"I will. See you in the lobby in a few."

She walked away from him and wondered what in the hell she was doing, maybe she should jump in her car and drive away as fast as she could. He could get a ride back, couldn't he?

CHAPTER 10

*S*teve couldn't believe they were actually getting a room and planning to have sex. He went into the locker room and looked in the mirror at his astonished face. This was either going to be awesome or it was going to be the worst mistake of his life. Well, next to marrying Katerina, and leaving Patsy high and dry, that is.

So, the second worst mistake of his life or the very best night. He had to make sure it ended up being the best. How he was supposed to do that he had no idea. But he couldn't just stand here looking in the mirror, that was for damn sure. He needed to go back to the little store for some condoms. He didn't have any with him, he hadn't thought there was any possible need to bring some with him to Colorado, let alone on their rock hounding trip.

He pulled on his jeans and t-shirt; he was not going shopping in his trunks. He got to the store and grabbed a hand basket. Might as well bring back a few more provisions for the night too. He needed to be quick though, he didn't want to keep the lady waiting.

The guy at the cash register looked up. "Let me know if you need any help finding something."

"Thanks, do you know if the lodge has room service?"

"Yes, pretty much around the clock. We sell some food too. In that room to your right." He waved toward the room he was referring to.

"Perfect, thanks, maybe I'll grab a few things just in case."

He got condoms, a couple of toothbrushes and toothpaste and some sweats for himself, if he knew Patsy, she would have an extra pair of clothes in her car, or maybe her pack. She had always been well prepared for every possible need. Then again, a lot of people in Colorado had a car full of items, for all eventualities, from eighty-degree weather to blizzards.

He looked quickly through the groceries and picked out some things that could work as either snacks or dinner, depending on how things went. He knew there was some food left from lunch too, if she brought it in. They should be fine between that, what he bought, and room service. He'd learned a long time ago that starving women was not a good idea. He had two sisters.

He was just finishing checking in when she came back in the lobby with her backpack. She'd put her hoodie on, and she looked pretty darn cute in her hoodie and towel.

"I got us one of the little cabins on property, I had my choice of pretty much anything. It's early for tourists and late for skiers, especially since there wasn't much snow this year."

"Yeah, not too surprised, the parking lot's not exactly full, now that the day people are gone. I brought the Rav over closer to the building. Looks like you bought out the store." She nodded towards his bags.

"Just a few items to get us through the night. They do have room service though, if we want to order something. Even in the cabins."

"I brought in the rest of the food from lunch, and I have stuff in my pack too. Don't want you to starve."

He laughed; it was funny to him that they both were thinking the same thing with concern for the other. As they got closer to the cabin, he started feeling nervous. Patsy was too important to bungle this. He'd not been very active sexually since his disaster of a marriage, and Katerina cheating on him had shook his confidence. Did he suck in bed, is that why she had cheated? He thought he left his partners fulfilled, but what if they were just faking it, like in that movie.

Well, he was going to do his damnedest to make sure Patsy didn't need to fake it; unless he totally chickened out and ran for the hills. They went into the cabin; it was a cozy two room space. The front room had a mini kitchen and eating area on one side, and a small living area with a fireplace and TV on the other. The fireplace was laid with wood, and paper sticking out in front in three locations, that nearly shouted 'light here'. If they were staying longer, or if they needed to stall, it would be a good plan to start the fire.

The front of the cabin had a picture window that probably had an awesome view in the daylight, but now it was all dark. He set his bags on the table and drew the curtains shut over the window. Patsy started putting the food he'd bought into the fridge. She just set the toothbrushes, giant economy box of condoms, and sweats to the side with no comment, although he did notice a small smile on her face.

The little store was well equipped with condoms. He'd decided they had more variety of those than they did food choices. Guess it was a hot selling item. All that fresh air and exercise from skiing in the winter and hiking in the summer.

Or maybe it was just lots of tourists hooking up with other tourists. Like a spring break fling, kind of scenario.

He let her finish with the food and took the other things into the bedroom, it had a large four-poster king-sized bed with a pretty quilt on it, unusual for a hotel, but it looked right in the cabin. The design looked like a columbine flower. He put the toothbrushes in the bathroom, that had a huge jacuzzi type tub, big enough for two, at least. And a shower that a whole family could enjoy, at the same time, it had water jets all around. He laughed, the "cabin" might look primitive from the outside, but the bathroom was amazing.

Patsy came in. "What are you laughing... oh my God look at this bathroom. I could spend a week in here, this is not at all what I was expecting from the humble little cabin."

"That's exactly what I was laughing about." He looked over at her and froze. She'd taken off her towel and hoodie and was standing there in that amazing swimsuit. He swallowed. "I appear to be over dressed."

"Yes, you are, I'm going to rinse off the hot springs in that amazing shower." She looked over her shoulder as she walked into the room. "Feel free to join me."

He just nodded dumbly.

"Hurry." She turned on the water and stepped into the spray.

He stumbled into the room and shucked off his clothes and grabbed a handful of condoms. The box tipped over and more tumbled out onto the floor, but he was in too big of a hurry to get back to Patsy to care. He could pick them up later.

Rushing back to the bathroom, he dropped the condoms next to the sink and stepped into the steam. Dear God, she'd shed her swimsuit and was standing under the streaming water naked and gorgeous. His fears and anxieties were swept away in a wave of pure lust. He was going to worship that beautiful woman, every inch of her, with his mouth, his hands and his body.

~

PATSY FELT THE SLIGHT BREEZE FROM STEVE STEPPING INTO the shower with her, she could nearly taste his desire, good thing, because she was ready to explode. If he even breathed in her direction, she was sure she would go off like a rocket.

She didn't want to admit it, but she'd been lusting after the man, since the first moment she'd walked into the restaurant for lunch with him. Then again it might have been from the moment she'd opened that damn email a month ago. Oh yeah, she was past primed for this.

She opened her eyes and there he was in all his masculine beauty, broad shoulders, muscled chest, narrow hips, strong defined arms and legs, and his erection, well it was magnificent. She remembered him being well endowed but... did they grow as you got older? Because she didn't remember him being quite so large.

"See something you like, beautiful?"

"Oh yeah, Steve, I do indeed. Get over here."

He grinned and moved in close. "Sorry I was frozen by your beauty; you are spectacular Patsy. Standing in the shower all wet with the steam rising around you, I thought I had walked in on a water goddess."

She put her hands around his neck, he slid his around her waist and pulled her in for a full body hug. She tilted her face up to him. "No flattery needed; this is a sure thing tonight."

"Not flattery, Patsy, pure unadulterated worship."

She giggled and rubbed her warm wet body against his. "Well in that case, worship away."

"Oh, I intend to," he said, right before his mouth came down on hers. Strong and needy, she opened to him and his tongue swept inside. She fought a duel with him, her tongue sliding along his, tasting him, fueling their passion.

He pulled her even closer, and she gripped his head, not giving him so much as a millimeter of freedom from her hungry mouth, not that he was resisting. Nope, he was right there with her just as greedy.

He finally broke the kiss and gulped in air, her lungs were burning too, so she didn't protest, but she didn't let go either.

He grinned down at her. "Trust me sweetheart, I'm not going anywhere."

She relaxed her hold on him a bit and he chuckled. Then he swooped in again, taking her mouth captive once more as he ran his hands up her back into her hair, tugged her head back and kissed his way down her exposed throat, hot open-mouthed kisses.

He licked and suckled and nipped as he went, and then started kissing his way back up her neck to her right ear, and bit gently on her earlobe. Fire shot through her body and pooled between her legs.

She caressed his shoulders and back, then ran her fingers down and gripped his ass with both hands. Trying to relieve the ache she ground her pelvis against him. He kissed across her cheek and nose and over to the other ear, took that lobe into his mouth and suckled. More fire shot through her and she thought she might go up in flames.

Why there was still water in the shower was beyond her, the lava flowing between them should be evaporating it, faster than it could come out of the jets.

He kissed his way down her neck to her shoulder and

sucked on the soft spot between them, she moaned. He let go of her hair and ran his hands down her back to her ass, as his mouth headed south to her breasts, that were more than ready for some attention. Her nipples were tight and hard, he circled the left one with his tongue and pulled it into his mouth and sucked gently.

This time lightning shot through her body igniting nerve endings, not just a few nerve endings, but every damn one of them. Her body felt like a live wire was attached. When he had tormented one breast he moved to the other and she just stood there unable to move from the electricity flowing through her body.

One of his hands stayed on her butt cheek while the other came forward and into her heat. His fingers parted her folds, and he caressed her, she dug her fingernails into his flesh and held on for dear life. He stroked her clit and then moved his hands back to put one, then two fingers inside of her, keeping the heel of his hand on her hot spot. She moaned, and he pulled his mouth off her breasts and crashed it back down on her mouth.

She came so hard she thought she might pass out from the feelings. Intense pleasure, almost to the point of pain, pounded through her veins. Patricia wasn't certain that lightning didn't shoot out of her fingers and toes. A scream echoed off the shower walls as the orgasm tore through her, and went on and on, wave after wave of sensation. She was sure she was going to die from the ecstasy, but then the sensations finally started to fade, and she lost all muscle control.

Steve picked her up and carried her to the bed, he must have grabbed some towels because when she could think again, she realized she was laying on some and he was wiping the water off her body with another. He pulled the sheets and blankets down on the other side of the bed, rolled her into it and covered her.

"I'll be right back. I have to turn off the water."

She made a noise in her throat, and even that was too much effort.

CHAPTER 11

*S*teve grinned, that had not been a fake orgasm, that's for damn sure. She could barely breathe; she'd come so hard. Her inner muscles had squeezed his fingers, and her body had gushed with her release. He'd practically come himself from the force of her orgasm. He turned to look in the mirror to make sure his ass wasn't bleeding from her digging her nails in. There were crescent shaped indents, but no blood. She had short nails, so that was probably the only reason he wasn't gushing blood.

He grabbed a condom and rolled it on, hoping he hadn't put her to sleep. Because he wouldn't want to wake her to slake his own lust. When he went back into the room and crawled in the bed next to her, she was on him in a flash. Nope, guess he didn't wear her out completely.

She crushed her mouth down on his and wriggled her way on top of him. She said, "That was amazing, but we're not finished yet, I want you inside me, now."

"Yes ma'am, I'm ready when you are." She slid her hand down to his cock and smiled as it jumped in her hand. Then she lifted up and guided him into her, she slid down taking him into her warm wet heat. Her body clenched his, she was so tight, and it felt so damn good, he thought he might die right there from the pleasure of her sinking down on him. She circled her hips and arched her back, and he slid in deeper.

And then she sighed, clenching her inner muscles on him and moving her hips just a little, giving herself pleasure and about killing him in return.

"Patsy, baby, can you move a little bit more?" he asked with gritted teeth.

She laughed a happy laugh. "Be my guest, Steve."

He groaned and rolled them both over, started moving inside her with long smooth strokes. She wrapped her legs around his hips, and he slid in even further.

"Mmm, that feels so good, Steve."

He picked up the speed a bit more, he didn't want her talking, he wanted her to be moaning or even screaming. He fit his mouth to hers and plundered, his tongue mimicking his body. She gripped his shoulders tighter, and he quickened the pace, he was determined to hold off his own release until she came again. She was meeting his strokes with her own, and she ground her pelvis against his.

He felt his own body gathering for release and tightened his muscles to hold off just a little longer. Her body started stiffening and he knew she was close; he tore his mouth from hers and moved to her ear and bit down lightly. She'd always had sensitive ears and that did the trick, she came with a scream and her body milked his. He gave in and joined her in the flames.

When he could think again, he realized he'd collapsed on top of her, and was afraid she couldn't breathe. So, he started to roll off of her.

She clutched onto him. "No, not yet, I like the feel of you right where you are."

"But you need to breathe too."

"I will, just wait a minute."

He nuzzled into her neck, kissing the soft skin there. She squirmed a little and patted his ass, he decided that was his cue to move off her. He rolled over and pulled out of her and got up to dispose of the condom in the bathroom.

She smiled sleepily at him. "Hurry back."

She was asleep when he got back from the bathroom, so he crawled in next to her and took her in his arms. She snuggled into him, and he marveled at the turn of events this day had taken. He'd had no idea what to expect this morning, but for tonight he was content to hold her, it felt like he'd come home after a long absence.

He thought about his past and how things might have been so different if he'd made other choices. But that was the thing about looking at the past, it all looked so cut and dried and clear and obvious. While you were in the middle of it though it was anything but.

Even now with this sweet interlude with Patsy, he had no clue about how the future would unfold, he still had a job and his entire family in Virginia, and Patsy had her job and some of her family here in Colorado. He didn't see much future for the two of them, but he was determined to enjoy the week he was here. He let his mind drift, and his body relax, he fell asleep with a smile on his face and a warm woman by his side.

PATRICIA WOKE SLOWLY, RELUCTANT TO LET GO OF SLEEP AND the pleasant dreams she was having of being with Steve again. As consciousness flowed into her, she realized that all those pleasant thoughts were not just dreams. She was being held firmly by Steve. Her head was on his shoulder, and her hand was on his chest over his heart. Their legs were tangled together. He was deliciously warm, and she felt so relaxed and content in his arms.

They'd had sex last night, several times, they had woken twice more and had been frantic for each other, and she wasn't quite sure how she felt about that. The actual act had been awesome; he had played her body like a fine instrument, tuned just to him.

She didn't remember their previous encounters as being quite so earth shattering, but they had been in their twenties, ten years did make a difference. Back then their lovemaking had been quick and strong and if truth be told a bit on the selfish side. She hadn't felt that way this time, it had been slow and purposeful, and well, let's just say it, amazing. So physically she was well sated and content with the experience. But emotionally, that was a different story.

He was only in town for a week and then he would be going back to Virginia. She didn't want any kind of emotional connection with him, she didn't want his leaving to break her heart. So, she needed to lock her feelings up tight. No emotions, no strings, just like she'd said last night. The question was, could she really do it.

She had two choices, run away from this immediately and close off her heart, or enjoy the sex and companionship while it lasted. Her body wanted the latter and her heart screamed for the former. She felt Steve start to wake up, she had maybe thirty seconds to decide. He started running his hand down her back and kissed her forehead and the decision evaporated in desire. Maybe she could indulge one last time before she put her foot down.

She let him carry her into the heat and passion. They

lingered and they savored—each touch, each kiss, each caress. The passion built slowly until it was an unstoppable force, when he finally entered her, she was so primed for him it felt like he belonged there.

She was certain when they exploded together, their release must have registered on the seismographs in the National Earthquake Information Center in Grandville. She inwardly chuckled at the thought, still a geologist through and through,

She drifted in the afterglow, her mind wandering, her body cooling. Steve had flipped them, so she was on top and he remained inside her, so there was no rush to part. It was delicious, he stroked her back and her head rested on his shoulder. Contentment filled her, and she thought it would be delightful to stay like this forever. But no this was not a forever kind of condition, and she might as well get that established right now.

She raised up and he looked at her. "I'm going to have a hot bath in that giant tub, and after that we probably need to get going."

"I can join you."

She shook her head. "No, I need a few minutes alone."

His eyes registered the hurt and disappointment he must have felt from her words. "Oh, well, I can keep myself occupied, I suppose."

"Great," she said as she lifted off from him. "If you want to use the bathroom before I go in there, now is your chance."

While he went into the bathroom, she gathered up clothes and toiletries, packed up the stray articles from their night together and tried not to wish things were different. When he walked out, she slipped in and locked the door. She needed this time to get her head on straight.

He'd started the hot water running into the tub, there were

some bath oil and bath bead samples on the shelf above the faucet, she selected one to pour in the hot water filling the tub. What a heavenly scent, she might just buy some for her own house, pretty clever of the makers to put some out next to that amazing tub.

She eased her sore body into the tub with steaming hot water. The soreness was not from their rock hounding, but from all the amorous activity, it had been a very long time since she'd had relations and even then, it hadn't been anything near the marathon she and Steve had put on last night. It was as if they were making up for lost time, or storing it up for the future, maybe both. Her body and her heart needed a break, which is also why she had insisted he find something else to do.

She needed some space and some time to get her head on straight before she let him slip further into her heart. He'd torn down some of her defenses and she needed to shore them up before they spent the next two hours in the car, and the week living in each other's pocket. Maybe during the summit, she could avoid him better. She would certainly have to attend the general assemblies, but she didn't need to go to his workshops, she could go listen to other people.

Although she had to admit his topic sounded fascinating, his team was trying out the new microbe technology, with some of the smaller mine reclamations they were working on. The big mines had to build a water treatment plant, but they were so expensive that the world's scientists had been working on a way to clean up smaller bodies of water, where a full-scale water treatment plant wasn't warranted, and it was impossible to deviate the water flow away from the mine. There were over five hundred thousand mines in the US, that needed help cleaning up the environment, so there was much work to be done.

Well, she could still go see other workshops even if his topic was one of the most interesting. She needed her peace of mind more than learning about the new technology.

CHAPTER 12

*S*teve thought he could go down to the gym to stretch out his muscles, the digging had left him a little sore. So, while Patsy had her alone time, he would get in a bit of a workout. He didn't stay long, just enough to warm up his muscles and work into a sweat. He hoped Patsy was not going to close down on him, but that sure seemed to be the case. He needed to think of a way to keep her off balance, so she wouldn't shut him out.

He decided to go back to the room and order breakfast, he was starving, and he was certain she would be too. But rather than showering in the gym, he decided to shower in their room, sometimes women liked a sweaty man. If he remembered correctly, Patsy was one of those women. He called room service, and they had just delivered the food when she came out of the bathroom.

He thought he saw desire flair in her eyes for just a moment; before she shut it down and focused on the food. He couldn't really blame her for that, because he was famished too. They had never gotten around to eating dinner last night.

During one of their sexcapades in the middle of the night they had stopped long enough for a naked picnic in bed. Made up from the food he'd gotten from the little store and the things she'd brought in from the car. But it hadn't taken long for them to move from food back to sex.

He'd gone a little wild in the breakfast ordering department, so there was probably enough food for six people, but they could always pack some with them for the drive back. The scents emanating from the different dishes as he uncovered them made his stomach clench and his mouth water. There was cinnamon French toast, bacon and sausage, eggs benedict, fresh pastries, hot coffee and three kinds of juice, because he couldn't decide on just one.

"Oh, thank God, I'm so starving I thought I might not make it out of the tub and dressed. You must have heard my stomach grumbling."

He shook his head. "Believe me, mine was screaming in protest too. I may have gone a little crazy ordering, but…"

"No, I don't think so, in fact there might not be anything left for you." She laughed and started loading up her plate.

He grabbed his dish and started doing the same. "Oh, no you don't, miss piggy."

They ate like ranch hands and washed it all down with plenty of coffee and juice. There was food left over, but not nearly as much as he had feared. When he couldn't eat another bite, he stood up and stretched. He noticed her eyes kind of glaze over. *Good, she's not immune to me, yet, anyway.* "I'm going to take a hot shower and get dressed."

She blinked and looked up to his face. "Um okay, I'll just, um, pack up everything. Yeah, pack up."

He grinned as he walked away from her to the bathroom. His strategy was working, and he had to keep her guessing.

She had a strong will, but he had one too. The battle was on, and it was the most fun he'd had in years.

~

Patsy breathed a sigh of relief when Steve shut the door. When she had walked out from her bath, and he was all sweaty and delicious looking, she'd almost caved. Fortunately, he had ordered breakfast. The coffee and food had called to her, so she could deliberately ignore the hot, sweaty, sexy, yummy, man.

She had worked hard to focus on her food instead of all those muscles across the table from her. Feeding one hunger and deliberately ignoring the other. Until he had stood and stretched before going to shower, his muscles had rippled, and his skin had gleamed, and she had nearly drooled. You would think they were teenagers the way they kept going at each other.

She shook her head at the thought, well no more of that, they were going back to professional associates, immediately. She just had to keep her eyes off his sexy self, fortunately the drive would keep her occupied. She waited for him to turn off the water and called out that she was going to carry some stuff to the car, and he could bring the rest and meet her outside. That would keep her from seeing him all warm and damp from the shower.

She got everything in the Rav, and he brought out the last few things, she managed to keep her back to him most of the time. She hadn't counted on him smelling so great when they climbed into the car for the drive back. Dammit she managed to keep one sense under control, and he'd snuck in with another. She glanced over at him and he looked so relaxed and adorable in his tourist clothes. He was wearing some sweats he'd purchased last night that had the Colorado flag on one peck.

She laughed at him. "Well, hello mister tourist."

"These were the least touristy sweats in the whole store. I didn't really want my whole back to have a picture of the hot springs, the Rockies, or columbine and aspen trees. This little flag was by far the sanest choice."

"But better than the dirty clothes from last night." She steered the car out of the resort and onto the highway.

"Much."

The drive back was uneventful, they talked and listened to music, and she didn't mind the silences, they were comfortable. But she tried to determine how to let Steve know they were done with the sex.

He wasn't a guy that would ever force a woman, so she just needed to let him know she was done with it. But she wanted to make it perfectly clear, so he didn't think she was acting strangely, and she didn't want him to think he should continue to pursue her. Maybe just the direct approach, he was a straightforward kind of guy.

When they got close to campus she said lightly, "That was an awesome weekend with you Steve, but I expect to proceed on a professional level for the rest of the week you are here."

Steve slowly turned his head. "Professional level?"

"Yes, colleagues, nothing more."

"As in no more sex, is that what you're saying?"

She nodded. "Exactly."

"Do you really think that's going to happen, we've been going at it like rabbits." He scoffed.

She said primly, "I do, we are adults and can control our baser instincts."

He laughed out loud. "All right professor, we can try it your way."

"Are you making fun of me?" She frowned at him, this was not a joke, she needed distance and no more intimacy.

"Yeah, a little. I just don't see how after making love for hours and hours, we're just going to turn off all that passion, or lust, or whatever you want to call it. We already tried holding that off, and it didn't work out so well." Then he smiled a slow sexy smile. "Actually, it worked out amazingly, but not the way you want to go forward."

Patricia sighed. "Well, you do have a point, but we aren't going to be alone either, we'll be busy with the summit and talking to all the people attending. So, we won't have as much temptation."

"Until we leave all those people and activities and come back to your cozy house for eight or so hours."

She frowned at him as she turned the corner to her street. "We'll be tired and need to sleep and check email and, and… stuff."

He grinned. "Stuff? Yeah, I guess there will be some *stuff*. I think a hot make-out session would be much more fun than *stuff*." He waggled his brows at her.

"More fun maybe, but also more dangerous." Shit did I just say that? He doesn't need to know I'm afraid of more intimacy. That's my own private business. Can I take it back without him wondering what's really going on? Or should I try to pass it off as a joke?

"Dangerous?" He shook his head. "No, we can be careful with condoms. I'm clean too, so no worries about STDs. After I found out my wife was cheating on me, I got fully tested and then checked again a year or so later, just to make sure she hadn't given me something. So, nothing dangerous to worry about."

Whew. Dodged the bullet that time, he thought I was talking about physical danger, not emotional. But it also pissed her off that he'd had to worry about getting something from his wife, that was supposed to be one of the perks of being married, that sex was safe.

God what a bitch he had married, stupid man. But she couldn't let herself feel bad for him, she needed distance and if she felt bad for him, she would want to make him feel better and down that road lay danger. No breaking it off was the way to go. "That's true, but condoms can break or not work properly."

She drove into her driveway and turned off the car, thankful to be able to talk about something else. "Let's get this all unloaded. We should probably clean up the minerals, so they can be nice and dry before you pack them to take with you."

"Changing the subject. Fine, I can do that. I would like to see them all cleaned up. I think we got some good specimens."

"I think so too. Want to order a pizza for dinner?"

"Does the Mexican place deliver, or can we grab take out? I've been thinking of their Colorado sauce since Jamal called me a month ago. I figure I need to eat it at least twice before I leave."

She laughed. "It is the best. I don't think they deliver unless they have one of the students working on the weekends, but they have takeout for sure. We could also order the frozen margaritas, they come virgin, but I have some tequila and a blender to mix it in with."

"Sold. Do you have them on speed dial?"

"That's a silly question, of course I do."

He grinned. "You are my kind of woman, Doctor Patricia Decatur."

She turned away and started into her house. She had been his kind of woman ten years ago, before he went off with

Katerina and broke her heart. Well, she wasn't letting him back in there, he'd lost that position in her life.

Fool me once and all that. Nope not going to be his kind of woman. She knew he was just talking about food, but that statement was a sore subject for her. Nope, she refused to be his kind of woman, that ship had sailed, and he'd missed the boat.

CHAPTER 13

*D*ammit, Patsy had retreated from him. He knew he shouldn't push her, he was only here for a week, but the last forty-eight hours had been the best two days he'd had in a very long time. And the last twenty-four might just take first place in his whole life.

He wished they didn't live so far apart. Was there any way to work out the distance, so they could have a real relationship? That was the question wasn't it. She had planned to join him in Virginia ten years ago, after she finished her PhD, but now she was settled in as a professor. If he didn't need to be in Virginia for his family, he might consider moving here.

But his parents depended on him to help out. His father was getting less mobile, so Steve went over nearly every weekend to see if his dad was planning any around-the-house chores, that he could help him with. And he went to see his nephew at least once a week, with little Kevin's dad being deployed, Steve tried to fill the gap of male influence.

His sister was a great mom, but sometimes the little guy needed a bigger guy around to teach him things. Kevin was only four, so Steve kept it low-key, but he liked being around the boy. And his sister always gushed about how grateful she was that he came around as often as he did. If things were different... but they weren't.

He would still love to spend more time with Patsy intimately. What if she could come visit him on her breaks and he came to visit her on his vacations. She had spring break and winter break and summer—if she wasn't doing a field lab—and he had three or four weeks of vacation a year, depending on how he used his personal time. That was nearly a week a month plus the summer. Hmm, he'd have to give that some more thought.

He dropped his stuff in his room and grabbed some clean jeans. It was good to have the clean sweats to wear home, but they felt like workout clothes. He changed into some black jeans and a black t-shirt. And went back to find Patsy, so they could get started cleaning up the rocks.

He found her in the mud slash laundry room off the back. It had a big deep sink and about a mile-long counter. She had all kinds of rock and mineral cleaning supplies in bins along the back of the counter, brushes from soft to steel, tiny picks, bottles of acid, rags, pressurized air, and some little buffers.

There was also an area for testing the rocks to determine what they were, streak plates, glass plates, a few bottles of chemicals, a hardness scale, several hand lenses, and even some electronic testers. In the corners of the room were some machines, maybe a sonic cleaner and a small sandblaster, but he wasn't quite sure.

Half a library of reference books filled two bookcases to overflowing. She had quite the setup. He saw some less professional test kits, charts, and rock collections, she had probably used as a kid or teenager. He wondered if she kept them around for sentimental reasons, or if she still used them?

He looked back at the woman in the center of it all and

felt slightly overwhelmed by her. She looked so right in this room, strong and beautiful and exactly at home. "Wow look at you, professional rock goddess."

She rolled her eyes at him. "It's my job, Steve."

He just lifted an eyebrow at her and waited her out.

"And I love it." She laughed and shook her head. "I loved it when I was six and I have never gotten over it." Her eyes lit up with joy, like a kid on Christmas morning and it made him happy to see it.

He tugged on her hair. "And no reason that you should get over it."

She clapped her hands like that happy child. "Let's get to it."

"Just tell me what to do."

OH, SHE WANTED TO TELL HIM WHAT TO DO, AND IT HAD nothing whatsoever to do with rock cleaning. She did love it, she wasn't lying or even exaggerating, but when the man had walked in the room in those tight black jeans and t-shirt, her mouth had started watering.

The black t-shirt emphasized his muscular arms and it fit him like skin. The black jeans cupped him in all the right places. This was ridiculous, she could barely walk after their amorous activities last night, and here she was again lusting after him.

She had laid some of their collection out on the work bench, but she dragged her eyes off Steve, by looking in the pack where the others were. There already plenty to start with laid out, but she had to do something to keep her from jumping the man, or even drooling. Drooling was not pretty. And she'd been the one to call a halt to the carnal side of their association, not relationship, association only.

With her head down pretending to look intently into the bag she said, "Start with the ones on the bench, run them under the water in the sink and you can use a soft brush on them to start. Knock the loose dirt off. Let's run through all the ones we collected, doing that to start. When you've got them as clean as possible set them on the bench and I'll look at them to determine the next step."

"Your wish is my command."

And did he have to say things like that in his deep rumbling voice. Dammit anyway, why didn't he have a high squeaky voice and skinny arms. Couldn't she catch a break, ever. His voice just rumbled through her and made every nerve stand on end, well she was not giving in to it. They had rocks to clean and she was going to chain her mind to that task come hell or high water.

She set more rocks on the workbench and glanced over to see him working on the first one. He was gently washing it and rubbing the dirt away with his fingers. And she wanted those wet gentle fingers on her. No, no, no, should she turn on music, should she start a conversation, should she dunk her head in the cold water, should she run away? She had to get past this obsession and the sooner the better.

"Here's the first one." He laid the rock with its crystals on the workbench.

"Great." Finally, she had something to keep her busy. She set the bag down with the rest of their specimens and went over to her work bench. After that, she did get lost in her work.

"All done, how about I get us some dinner." She startled when he spoke, she'd been immersed in the rocks and had tuned everything else out.

"That would be great, I'll have the large burrito platter, ground beef with Colorado sauce and melted cheese. And a strawberry margarita. There's a menu in the drawer under the toaster oven."

"Perfect, after we eat you can show me what you've gotten cleaned up and identified."

"Sounds like a plan." She mumbled and went back to her rocks. She nearly didn't register him chuckling and walking out of the room.

~

STEVE LAUGHED AS HE WENT INTO THE KITCHEN. THAT woman could really focus in, when she was working on her beloved rocks. She'd nearly jumped out of her skin when he'd spoken. He'd even watched her for a couple of minutes before interrupting her.

It was fun to watch her so intent on the mineral specimens they had collected, she had strong hands and he'd enjoyed watching her scrub the sample she was working on, using the brushes and little picks to get to the beryl crystals. He'd noticed while washing them that they had nearly the full spectrum of colors and he wondered how large of an area her deposit ran.

He found the menu and called to order the food, they did have someone delivering tonight, but it was an hour wait, so he decided to just go pick it up himself. If he did that, he could have it in twenty minutes. He was starving, so picking it up was the better choice. They'd had a ginormous break-fast, but that had been hours ago.

He grabbed his wallet and keys and headed out, he debated telling Patsy, but she'd probably forgotten he was even in the house, let alone going to get food. He had a sneaking suspicion she would have just worked right through dinner, if he hadn't forced the issue.

He got to the restaurant and the familiar smells of cumin and roasted chilies assaulted him, along with the laughter from the bar area. It was a fun place, and many of the older students spent a lot of time in that bar. He and Patsy had spent their fair share once she'd finally turned twenty-one. They had eaten there before that, but the bar had been off limits.

One of the owners came out of the back room and smiled at him, she was a short woman with gray frizzy hair and snapping brown eyes. He remembered her from the past, she always spoke to her customers and made everyone feel welcome. She put her hands on her hips. "So, you're back in town, are you? Haven't seen you in nearly a dozen years."

He was shocked that she would still remember him at all. "Yeah, back for the energy summit. I live in Virginia now, but they asked me to come be the keynote."

"Nice. I have to admit; I was surprised when you didn't take Dr. Patricia with you when you left. She still comes in a lot or does take out. You guys were pretty tight back then, practically inseparable."

"Yeah, that was poor judgement on my part. I'm staying with her for the summit."

"Are you now? Well try not to break her heart when you leave this time."

He blinked at the old woman, he'd forgotten that part of her personality, she wasn't shy about letting you know if you were acting a fool. Now he remembered her hauling more than one six-foot burly engineer to the door by their ear and telling them to go home and sleep it off. Especially if they got out of hand with the waitresses, or any other woman in the restaurant. They served alcohol, but no one got away with abusing it, on her watch.

He didn't know what to say to her about breaking Patsy's heart when he left this time. He certainly didn't plan to break her heart, but he hadn't planned it the first time either. Maybe the point was that he needed to actually think about it this time, rather than making stupid assumptions.

He nodded. "I'll try my best ma'am."

"Good, because I would hate to have to hunt you down and give you a good ass whuppin'."

He shifted from foot to foot and wondered what to say to that, he was saved by the hostess bringing his food out.

But before he could get away, the owner put her hand on his face. "You take care now young man and come back and see me again." Then she bustled off to her next victim. Steve breathed a sigh of relief and paid for the food, while the hostess tried to hide her smile.

CHAPTER 14

*P*atricia was working on a particularly brilliant crystal formation when her stomach made itself known, as her nose detected a whiff of Colorado sauce, and she could also hear her blender going. She hadn't noticed she was famished, but that smell had wound its way into her, and she felt like that cartoon where the wolf—or whatever it was —floated on the scent. She totally had no power over her body as it put down the specimen, stood up and headed to the kitchen. She did manage to stop long enough to wash her hands, but that was it.

She walked into the kitchen. "Oh my God I'm starving, I'm so glad you got food. I wouldn't have come up for air until all those damn rocks were perfect."

He chuckled. "Yeah, I noticed, which is why I just left without saying anything. I kind of figured you wouldn't even notice I was gone."

She nodded and grabbed one of the containers pulling the lid off. "Are they the same?"

"No, I got carne asada and you got ground beef, so mine has a CA on the top and yours has a GB."

She flipped her lid over and saw the GB, yay for picking the right one. She seized a fork out of the drawer and then thought she should be polite and got Steve one too. There was sour cream in the fridge, so she pulled that out and took it all over to the breakfast bar. She probably should be gracious and wait for Steve, but he was busy playing bartender. There were some pockets of chips and the restaurant's homemade salsa, so she decided to have a few of those while he finished the drinks, but he better hurry, because she wasn't waiting forever.

The chips were still slightly warm, and she dug deep into the salsa to load up the chip. She put it in her mouth and the flavor exploded on her tongue. The perfect amount of spice with the fresh taste of the tomatoes and onions was delicious. She moaned her appreciation and then took another chip. She looked up at Steve. He was standing there staring at her with a drink in each hand.

"What?"

"No moaning, dammit. I'm having a hard enough time not jumping you, no sex noises."

She laughed. "I'll try to keep the sex noises to a minimum, but I'm starving, and the salsa is excellent, it just sneaked out."

"Well, no more. No moaning, groaning, whimpering, or sighing." He set their drinks down, then sat and opened his takeout container. Then he moaned, just from the smell.

All her senses went on alert and she knew exactly how he felt. She wagged her fork at him. "If I can't moan, neither can you."

He winked at her. "I'll try to control myself, if you do the same."

"Deal." She loaded her fork with a huge bite of her burrito, the Colorado sauce and cheese dripped off as she stuffed it in her mouth. This time she managed—just barely —not to moan. The smooth coolness of the sour cream enhanced the spicy beef and tangy sauce.

Steve took his first bite, and she could practically see him holding in the groan of appreciation. What a pair they were. She reached for her margarita and the icy sweet strawberry flavor tangled with the bite of tequila as she sipped it. Again, she fought the sex noises, as Steve had called them. Eating a delicious meal in silence was nearly impossible.

She looked up at him and he was watching her intently. "What? I didn't make any noises."

"No, but you wanted to, and your face is very expressive."

"Too bad. You are just going to have to get over it, because this is delicious and your ban on noises is ruining half the fun."

"Fine, moan away, but I'm going to too."

"Fine." She took another bite of burrito and let her appreciation loose verbally.

They spent the rest of the meal trying to outdo the other in enjoyment of their food and laughing like loons, which fortunately broke the sexual tension, and they could enjoy their meal.

When she got up to put her dishes in the dishwasher and get rid of the trash, her head spun a little and she thought maybe the alcohol had contributed to the relaxed meal. Steve must have been very liberal with the tequila.

"Woah, put a little tequila in those margaritas, didn't you? Are you trying to get me drunk?"

He grinned at her. "Would it help?"

"Help put me to sleep, yes, yes it would. Help you get me naked? Only if I want you to."

He shrugged. "It was worth a try. But no, I really didn't

do it for that reason, I couldn't find a shot glass, so I had to guess."

"That makes sense. But you guessed a little on the heavy side, which means we're done cleaning the rocks for tonight. I don't want to damage them or myself, those picks are sharp." She held out her hand and pointed to a scar on her middle finger.

He took hold of her hand and gently kissed the scar. Fire raced through her, that had nothing to do with the spicy food they had eaten, and everything to do with the man holding her hand.

"Poor finger, looks like it might have needed stitches."

She just stood there unable to speak. Until he looked up and she was certain he could see the lust in her eyes. She was nearly trembling with it.

"Um, Patsy?"

"To hell with the no more sex thing. We can do no more sex, when you go back to Virginia."

"Which I'm already dreading. But I don't want to take advantage of you after that margarita." He stroked his thumb over her palm.

"It was one maybe two shots at the most. Nothing to take advantage of. Or maybe I'll take advantage of you."

"But you said…"

She shook her head. "I said that sharp instruments should not be used after having a couple of drinks. Not that I can't think or make decisions."

"But will you be angry with me, or yourself in the morning, that's the real question."

She thought about it, would she be disappointed in the morning? She looked at the man in his black jeans and tight black t-shirt. The t-shirt that enhanced his broad shoulders and muscular arms, and was tight enough she could see the muscle definition in his chest and abs. The strong hands that held hers so tenderly. The black jeans that cupped his ass and his sex and strong legs. His dark brown hair flopped over his forehead and his sky-blue eyes looking deep into hers. His mouth was set in a grim line of determination, the beard around it making him look almost fierce.

"Nope, not going to be disappointed in the morning. Not unless you turn me down."

"Do I look stupid?" he asked in amazement. He pulled her close to him with the hand he still held and wrapped his other arm around her back. "Turning you down is so far out of the realm of possibilities, that I can't even imagine it."

"Good, then stop talking and kiss me." She reached up with her free hand, tangled her hand in his hair and drew his face down.

He met her with a greedy kiss. She rejoiced in the flames that rose up to sear them both. He tasted like Colorado sauce and tequila and Steve. Mostly like Steve, and that taste far outweighed the man-designed tastes, of the food. Warmth spread through her body as their tongues tangled and played.

STEVE WAS HAPPY TO COMPLY WITH HER DEMANDS FOR A kiss, he'd never been in such a state of constant arousal. Since the day she'd walked into that Italian restaurant he'd been hard to semi hard the entire time. Had it really only been two days. Only forty-eight hours, well more like fifty-five hours now, but still he didn't think that was possible, so much had changed since that first chilly reception.

He wanted nothing more, than to bury himself inside her and never come out. How could he be so addicted to her, after such a short time. And how in the hell was he going to leave her in a week. He had no idea. But for now, for today and every day she would have him, he was going to enjoy every single second.

He kissed her until he had no breath and then he moved his mouth to her neck, and kissed his way down that soft warm skin to her shoulder. "Oh Patsy, you taste like heaven, ambrosia maybe. God girl, I can't get enough of you."

She moaned as he sucked on the soft spot between shoulder and neck. His whole body ignited with the sound, so he bit the spot lightly and then soothed it with his tongue. She dug her nails into his neck and rubbed her pelvis against him. He needed skin, so he dragged her long sleeve t-shirt off her. He groaned because under that was a tank top.

"Too many clothes."

She nodded. "Yeah, but it was cold in the mountains, so layers were a requirement."

Pulling at her tank, he dragged it out of the top of her jeans and up over her head. She raised her arms to help. Skin, soft and smooth and warm. He ran his hands up her arms and then down her torso to her waist. Velvet smoothness met his fingers and he decided nothing felt better than Patsy's skin under his hands.

"So soft, so beautiful." Claiming her mouth with his, he let his palms run up her ribcage to the bottom of her sports bra, his knuckles grazed the undersides of her breasts. She shivered and then went to work on his t-shirt, pulling it loose and pushing it up his body. He grabbed the back of it with one hand, hauled it over his head, and threw it to the side where her clothes had landed. They were getting quite a pile on the kitchen floor. Kitchen.

"Do you want to take this somewhere other than the kitchen?" he asked.

"Too far, do you have a condom in your jeans? Because I'm going to cry if we have to hunt one down."

"Yes, I have one in my jeans. Again, do I look stupid?"

"No not stupid, just making sure you were still hopeful, about me changing my mind."

"Always hopeful where you're concerned. And I would hate to disappoint you and make you cry, while I hunt them down." He smiled at her.

"Yay, then what are you waiting for, get it out and lose those jeans."

She yanked her sports bra off and started unzipping her own pants and he was frozen, watching all that skin appear. She pushed her jeans and panties to the floor and kicked them to the side.

She looked up at him and narrowed her eyes. "Hey, you're supposed to be naked too."

"I couldn't move, I was too busy watching your beautiful body being revealed."

She blushed. "But now I'm naked and you're not, I don't normally stand around in my birthday suit in my kitchen. So, unless you are trying to ruin the mood, lose the clothes, buster."

"Yes ma'am." He took the two condoms in his pocket out and handed them to Patsy.

She raised her eyebrows, but didn't say anything while he quickly stripped off the rest of his clothes. He lifted her up and set her on the kitchen table, took one of the condoms and rolled it on. But then he decided that he needed to slow this down a little, so he started playing with her breasts, lifting the weight of them and running his thumbs over the nipples. She whimpered, so he squeezed her nipples, gently teasing them into a tight bud.

He took one of the tight buds into his mouth and let his

hand drift down between her legs. The wetness there indicated she was ready for him, he moved his mouth to her other breast to suckle that nipple. Then kissed his way down her side. He knelt on the floor and pulled her to him, he just needed a taste of her.

"Steve…"

"It's good baby, I just need a small taste." He licked her gently, she tasted amazing. She squirmed as if trying to get away from him, but he lifted her legs and put them over his shoulders, and anchored her hips with one hand, then he licked her again. "Lay back a little sweetheart."

"Oh my God, what are you doing."

"Just having a little dessert," he said, with his mouth up against her and she squirmed more. "Lean back on your elbows."

PATRICIA LEANED BACK AS HE ASKED, AND THOUGHT SHE WAS going to die from what he was doing to her. She'd heard of this, certainly, but she'd never experienced it. He was holding her open with one hand and licking her. It was the most erotic feeling ever. She'd always thought it sounded disgusting, but it sure didn't feel disgusting, it felt amazing.

He started sucking on her and then he put one finger inside her, then a second. He rubbed gently on a spot inside, while he sucked on what felt like the same spot on the outside. She couldn't fight the sensations building in her, she gripped the edges of the table as the most intense orgasm she'd ever had, ripped through her body. She felt it in every cell. He slowed his assault but didn't stop. He gentled his touch, so the feelings lessened, but the gentle waves kept flowing through her.

She sighed and lay down on the table unable to move. He took her legs off his shoulders and picked her up and carried her to his bed. He laid her gently on his bed and climbed into it with her.

She managed to roll her head to look at him. "That was amazing."

He grinned. "I'm here to please."

"Well in that case, continue on." She waved her hand and moved her legs apart in invitation. He didn't hesitate to obey her command. He moved between her legs and entered her slowly. She felt her body open to accommodate his size. He filled her up and it felt divine. To urge him on, she wrapped her legs around his waist, and he moved in deeper than before.

He pulled back and then filled her over and over with strong smooth strokes. She felt her body start to gather again and he hit just the right angle. She gripped his arms with her hands, and he kissed her as he kept the movement up. He filled her in every way, as his mouth mimicked the long smooth strokes. She tightened her grip with both arms and legs.

When she got close to a second release she said, "Now come with me."

He groaned and they both came at the same time. He stayed on top of her just the way she loved it, until she tapped him on the shoulder, he kissed her neck and pulled out.

"I'll be right back."

"I'll be waiting."

Patricia scooted over a little, so Steve could crawl in next to her. She should probably go to her own room, but she enjoyed sleeping with the nice warm man, and she only had a few days to enjoy him, so why should she deny herself the joy of sleeping in his arms.

He came back in the room and crawled into bed with her, pulling the covers up over the top of them. He drew her into his arms and kissed her gently, then laid her head on his shoulder.

"Will you stay with me?" he asked.

"Yes, I will."

"Perfect."

CHAPTER 15

*P*atsy felt wonderful in his arms, he could stay like this all night.

Suddenly she sat straight up. "Fuck, what time is it?"

"Maybe seven, seven thirty, why?"

"The mixer is tonight, we have to get dressed and get over there, right now. Thank God, we decided to do it after dinner. I'm on the committee and we don't know how Jamal is feeling, I need to be there before it opens at eight. And you're the keynote and need to be there too."

He groaned. "Well, damn. I suppose you're right." He snagged his tablet off the nightstand and swiped his finger over it. "Seven twenty-five."

She scooted out of bed. "Good, I'm getting dressed, I'll meet you in twenty minutes."

"I could call Jamal…"

"No, we both need to go, whether he is better or not. Move it mister."

He flopped back in bed when she scurried out the door. *Well shit, I had her right where I wanted her.* He shook his head and got up to get ready

When he walked into the front room, he stopped short and was sure he stopped breathing. She was standing there in a killer dress of deep royal blue, it was fitted on top with a scoop neck, there was a belt at the waist, and then it flared out at the bottom ending right above her knees. Strappy sandals with heels, made her legs look miles long. Her hair was twisted up in a fancy knot and she'd put on makeup. She had on a necklace, earrings and bracelet of lapis lazuli that looked like custom designed jewelry, and he wondered if she'd found those stones on a field trip.

He finally got his brain and feet moving again, he took her hand and kissed it. "You look wonderful. Did you find these stones?"

She laughed. "Yes, in Crested Butte, but not on the ground, I bought the stones in a shop and had Kristen, my friend in Washington, set them for me, I love her work."

"It's very beautiful and looks great with this dress, and the whole thing makes your eyes stand out. It almost makes them look blue."

"I know, that's part of the reason I bought it, my normally boring gray eyes look so much brighter."

He shook his head. "Your eyes are beautiful, nothing boring about them at all."

"Thank you." She stammered and blushed. "But we better get going."

"I'll drive, so we don't have to walk back in the dark."

They parked behind the building where the reception was being held and went in the back door, since Patsy had a key to it. The building was built on a hill, so the back door was down lower than the main entrance, but the reception was being held in the ballroom that was on the lower level. They went in through the service area where the caterers were able to unload food and drinks. That was all finished, so they weren't in the way. They noticed the setup was proceeding as planned.

She would come back and check on things later, but she wanted to get into the ballroom to see what it looked like first. Next to the service area, there were a dozen ten-top round tables, set up with tablecloths and flowers in the center. This would be the quiet area where people could sit, talk and network. The ballroom space with the wood floor would have music and people would be moving around to socialize. There was a bar off to the side for people to get drinks. No one could get in that wasn't registered for the summit, so it was an open bar. Once they got into the main dance floor area they saw Jamal, still looking a little pale, but among the living. They walked up to him.

"Jamal, you're here."

"Steve, my friend, yes I finally got to feeling better. At least good enough to come in, the rest of the family is on the mend also."

Steve shook his friend's hand, and noticed Jamal looked a little unsteady. He was trying to figure out what to say to get him to sit down for a minute, when Patsy spoke up.

"I'm so glad to hear that, but you still look a little pale, why don't you and Steve sit down over there, and I will check on everything." She waved toward a table.

"That might be a good idea Patricia, I'm not quite a hundred percent yet." Jamal grimaced and Steve smiled at her letting her know he appreciated her stepping in. He was grateful she had noticed and knew what to say.

"You two have a lot to catch up on, have a seat and I'll do the running," she said, steering them toward a table. "And when I'm done, I'll bring over some drinks."

"Just water for me, thanks Patricia." Jamal patted his stomach.

Steve said, "I wouldn't mind a beer."

"Perfect, I'll be back in a few." She started off toward the DJ.

Jamal smiled at him. "So, it looks like you two are doing good, she's not glaring daggers at you, anyway."

"We've had some time to talk things through. I hurt her pretty bad ten years ago, but she's a loving and forgiving person."

"Patricia is a good woman. I've always been surprised that no one else has snapped her up. She's dated a few guys, but it never seemed to last long. And I have to admit, I heard some grumbling about her shutting them down."

Steve didn't like the idea of her being with other men, but he's the one that got married, so he had no right to lay claim on her whatsoever. "She's a beautiful woman, it wouldn't surprise me that the guys wanted to be with her. So, they probably didn't take well to her ending their relationship."

"Some of the grumbling was more about her being an ice princess with a heart of stone. So, it didn't seem like your normal end of a relationship. It sounded to me like it never was a real union. That she wouldn't let them into her heart or her bed. But I don't know that for sure, since I didn't feel it was my place to ask."

Steve was surprised to hear that, because Patsy had not acted like the ice princess with him, in any way. Oh, their first meeting was chilly, but once they'd talked that first night she'd been her normal warm self, and there was nothing icy about their time in bed, on the contrary the woman was pure fire. Not that he was going to explain that to Jamal.

He shrugged and decided to change the subject. "Just sour grapes, I think. So, tell me about your family. Did I see you have a boy and a girl?"

Jamal smiled and was off talking about his kids, he got

out his phone to show Steve picture after picture of them. Relating stories that indicated that the girl was quite a little hellion and the son who was the eldest was quiet and reserved, who felt it was his duty to take care of his little sister.

Steve enjoyed the tales, and it was clearly one of Jamal's favorite topics.

PATRICIA CHECKED ON THE MUSIC THAT WOULD START playing when the doors were opened. She made sure the main doors were manned by some grad students, there were a lot of people waiting on the porch for admittance into the lobby. The sign-in people were in place, with name tags and conference packets.

Betty, an older woman who worked in the computer lab was looking frustrated, so Patricia went up to her. "Is there a problem?"

Betty nodded her head sending the gray chin length hair flying. "Oh, dear Patricia, the S to V list is missing. I know it was here, but now it's just gone. We need to open the doors, but we can't until it's found." She wrung her hands, and her hazel eyes filled with unshed tears. She turned and started going through all the folders on the table again. Sending the other two women to look in the transport boxes one more time.

Patricia looked around and noticed the second table, with the conference bags, was all neat and tidy except for one small area where the bags had avalanched. Patricia started to stack the bags up and found under the avalanche there was a folder just like the ones on the table. She flipped it open and sure enough it was the S-V list.

"Found it Betty." She handed the folder to the woman who nearly cried in relief.

"Oh, thank you Dr. Patricia, I don't know what we would have done without you."

"You would have found it, but I'm glad I could help. Give me five more minutes, then open the doors."

"Will do, thanks again," Betty cried out.

Patricia went back down the sweeping staircase to the ballroom, she always felt like a princess coming down those stairs. She imagined the staircase was designed like that for that very purpose. It was an impressive room and lots of the alumni and benefactor meetings were held there for fundraising.

She headed back to the catering area to make sure nothing was needed there. They were using a caterer that was one of their standard event vendors, so she didn't really expect any trouble, plus it was just snacks and desserts, so nothing elaborate, but she wanted to let them know to contact her if anything came up. Everything looked good there, so she grabbed a water bottle for Jamal, a beer for Steve and a hard lemonade for herself.

When she walked back to the table, she'd left Jamal and Steve at, she noticed there were people starting to come in from outside. She went over to Jamal and Steve and put their drinks down on the table.

Jamal stopped mid-sentence. "How is everything, is there something I need to do?"

"Everything is perfect, the check-in people were missing one folder, but we found it under some of the conference bags. So, everything is good to go, you can see people are starting to come in." She waved her hand toward the staircase. "You guys can just hang out here and let people come up to chat with you. Jamal, don't wear yourself out tonight, we've got a whole week to get through."

"Yes mother," Jamal said with a smile.

Steve grinned at her and she blushed. "I'm going to go um, check on…" she muttered and fled, leaving her hard lemonade on the table.

She had to get a grip; she couldn't go all school girl the instant that man smiled at her. Stupid blush, for God's sake she was thirty-three years old. Why was she acting like a twelve-year-old around him? Stammering, blushing, tingling at inappropriate times. She needed to get herself under control. Immediately if not sooner. She squared her shoulders and threw back her head and walked back into the crowd.

Patricia greeted people and smiled, pointing the way to the refreshments and anything else they asked about. Then she saw a fraternity sister coming down the stairs and made a beeline for her.

"Ramona, I'm so glad you could make it." She grabbed both hands and held them tight. Ramona was a short woman with lots of curves, who was always complaining about being overweight. Patricia thought that most men would think she was perfect. She had on a flirty dress of blue with a jacket over the top that was long. The flirty dress was consistent with Ramona's personality, but the jacket was not. She wondered if the jacket was meant to hide some of those curves. Patricia thought the insecurity and constant dieting was something left over from her marriage, she couldn't remember Ramona mentioning her weight, before she was with her ex.

Ramona laughed; she had a big laugh that drew attention. "Once I saw who the keynote was, I had no choice. I didn't want to miss the fireworks. So, did you castrate the poor guy yet?"

Patricia looked around quickly to see if anyone had heard the outspoken woman, and then dragged her off to the side. "I can't believe you said that."

"Are you kidding, half our class is coming just to see what happens between the two of you." She patted Patricia on the arm like she would a little kid or a dog.

"What?" she screeched and then she lowered her voice and pulled Ramona even further away from everyone else. "You're kidding, right?"

"Maybe exaggerating a bit, it's probably only a quarter of the class." She laughed out loud. "You should see your face; you're the color of a tomato. So, what have you and Mr. Sampson been up to anyway?"

"Nothing much." She looked away; something must need her attention. The only thing she saw was two more fraternity sisters bearing down on them. She groaned inwardly, what was she going to say to them. They had stood by her when Steve had gotten married, and her heart was broken. She couldn't just ignore them, so she stood up straight and plastered a huge smile on her face.

"Carol, Betsy, it's great to see you, thanks for coming." Carol was tall and had bright red hair, that today was perfectly straight and hung past her shoulders. It changed colors whenever Carol had a whim, and if it was allowed to be natural, it curled into long fat ringlets, the kind that other people paid hundreds of dollars to achieve. She had bright blue eyes with a green ring around the outside, and a wide smile. She wore a silk pantsuit of soft green and chunky jewelry.

Betsy was average height with black hair and nearly black eyes, she was Latino with gorgeous taupe skin, that went beautifully with the cream color belted dress and bold print jacket she had on tonight.

Betsy took her hand and looked her in the eye. "We had to be here to support you, since that rat is the keynote." Carol and Ramona nodded.

Shit, shit, shit. This was damn near an intervention, she had to clue them in before something happened. "Let's hit up the ladies' room and I'll explain." She started towards the restroom and then stopped short. "First, is there anyone else coming, because I would rather only go over this once."

Betsy shook her head, "Madeline is on tap if we need her, but she can't get away until Wednesday. Blanche said to call her if things started going badly, and she would fly in."

"From London? Are you kidding me?" Patricia couldn't believe her ears. "That's really sweet of you guys, but not at all necessary."

Carol put her hands on her hips. "*We* will be the ones to decide that."

They all went into the bathroom, it was a fancy setup with a small lounging area out front, so they settled in. Patricia told them all about why Steve had married Katerina and how their marriage hadn't gone so well. She hinted at it ending by his wife cheating on him and divorcing him. She didn't go into all the details but gave them enough information that they wouldn't kill Steve.

She told them about going rock hounding however she didn't go into all the details of the weekend. They didn't need to know about the sexcapades, but she did let them know that there had been some interest on both sides, and they were feeling their way along. She didn't need an intervention, or any of the other girls flying in to rescue her.

Betsy looked at Carol and Ramona and then nodded. "Fine we'll let this play out for now, but you'll let us know if we need to step in."

Patricia smiled. "I will, but I'll be fine."

"Until he leaves again," Ramona said crossing her arms over her chest and frowning.

"No, it's different this time, I know he's not here for good, so I'm prepared for him leaving. I love you guys for riding to my rescue. But there won't be a breakdown, one broken heart per lifetime is my quota, more than that is just redundant. Now, with Jamal just barely over the stomach flu, I need to get back out there, in case someone needs something."

They stood and she hugged each one of them, and they went out into the reception which was now in full swing. Someone tapped her on the shoulder, so she split off toward the DJ while the girls walked out into the crowd.

CHAPTER 16

Steve wondered where Patsy had gone off to, he'd seen her talking to Ramona who had been in her fraternity, but then someone had come up to speak to him and he didn't see where she went. He didn't need to keep tabs on her, but he just liked looking at her, watching her move and handle all the little things. Chatting with people and smiling.

He saw her and three of her sorority sisters come out of the hall where the women's bathrooms were. Someone tapped her on the shoulder, and she went off to help. Her three comrades looked at each other and then at him, and then they looked toward where Patsy had gone, they whispered to each other and nodded and then headed toward him. *Oh shit, I am in trouble now.*

They stopped next to his table, Ramona and Carol crossed their arms and Betsy sat down next to him. He turned his full attention to Betsy, fortunately Jamal was chatting with another couple.

Betsy said quietly, "Patricia told us what happened, and she said she's fine with it. But we just want to let you know that if you break her heart again—like you did last time—we will hunt you down and castrate you. Do you understand?"

He cleared his throat. "I have no intention of hurting her."

Betsy spoke even quieter and somehow it was even more threatening. "Good because I meant what I said." Then her demeanor changed completely, and she smiled brightly at him. "It's good to have you as the keynote Steve."

The other girls smiled and nodded, having uncrossed their arms and he wondered what in the hell was going on, until he heard Patsy's voice behind him.

"You girls remember Steve, don't you?" She put a hand on his shoulder and reached around him to take up her hard lemonade.

Betsy smiled up at Patsy. "Sure, we're just letting him know how much we appreciate him coming back for this." Betsy looked back at him and narrowed her eyes. "It should be interesting to see how it goes."

Carol said, "Let's get some drinks, sisters."

When they walked away Steve breathed a sigh of relief, and Patsy sat down in the chair Betsy had vacated. "So, what did the girls want?"

He squirmed a little. "Oh, um just to say hi."

"Umm hmm, they were totally threatening you, weren't they?"

"Why do you say that?" Steve hedged.

"Well let's see, Betsy was all up in your grill with a menacing expression, Carol and Ramona were standing there with their arms crossed glaring daggers at you, and when I walked up, they were suddenly all smiles."

"Well, they were a little confrontational."

She laughed. "I can imagine, so did they threaten death and dismemberment?"

"Nope, just castration." He squirmed again.

"Oww, that's harsh. They seem to think I need protection from you."

"Yeah, I gathered that." He took her hand and rubbed her knuckles. "I don't want to hurt you Patsy. But I didn't the first time either."

"This time I know the score Steve, and I'm not a young woman with stars in her eyes. I'll be fine when you leave—to go back to your world."

He felt both relieved and saddened by what she said, he dearly wished he hadn't been the one to knock those stars out of her eyes. And it tugged at him—just a bit—that she thought she would be fine when he left, because he wasn't all that sure he would be fine—when he left her.

"So, I'm sorry the girls were harassing you."

He shrugged. "No worries Patsy. Don't they have their own husbands to harass?"

She laughed and shook her head. "Betsy yes, she's been married since graduation and has a couple of kids. Ramona is divorced, she was married a few years, but the guy was a real jerk, not physically abusive, but emotionally, it was a different story. They have a son and he wants nothing to do with him. She's got a good family though, so lots of support there. Carol is gay and has a life partner, they may get married now that it's legal in Colorado."

"Do they all live in the area?"

"Ramona and Carol do, Betsy lives on the eastern slope near Grand Junction."

"Is Betsy in the environmental engineering sector? I thought she was a computer geek."

Patsy looked away from him and fidgeted. "Yes, she's a software engineer."

"Then why did she come to this summit?"

"Well, um, to support me, since you're the keynote." Each

word got softer until he could barely hear what she was saying. He had to think about what she had said, since the last word was mouthed rather than spoken. He blinked and then burst out laughing.

"Seriously, she came just because I'm the keynote." He laughed again and then looked at Patsy who wasn't laughing. That sobered him. "They really are afraid for you, aren't they?"

She nodded.

"I see. They were here the first time around and it was more brutal than you've let on, wasn't it?"

She nodded.

"Well, hell. I'm so sorry Patsy, I wish I could go back and change things. I so callously hurt you and I had no idea. Can you forgive me?"

She nodded. Then she shrugged and smiled at him. "I already have, Steve. The girls on the other hand, not so much. It's always easier for the person that was really hurt to forgive, than it is for the people who have to watch."

PATRICIA NEEDED TO MOVE, THIS CONVERSATION WAS TOO much for a room full of people. She patted Steve's hand and pushed back her chair. "I need to do another round of checks."

Steve started to stand. "I can go with—"

She interrupted, she needed a minute alone. "No, you stay here with Jamal. I'll only be a minute or two."

He looked at her intensely, like he was reading her thoughts, then he shrugged and sat back down. "Okay, but I'm happy to help."

"No need, be right back." She turned and walked away quickly, breathing a sigh of relief as she went.

She made a circuit of the room, everything was running smoothly, they didn't need her. Which was partially a relief, and at the same time didn't give her any excuse to stay away for a few minutes. The girls being there, had brought back a lot more of the pain she had gone through ten years ago. She'd learned to bury the trauma of those days and didn't think about it.

Even when she'd heard Steve was coming, she'd managed to keep the real pain from that time from surfacing. But right now, it wasn't so easy to do, even though they had talked through the reasons the hurt was still there. She glanced back toward Steve, there were some people talking to him and Jamal.

She turned back around and nearly ran into Aaron Silverton. "I almost crashed into you." She smiled at him.

He looked at her like she was gum stuck to the bottom of his shoe. "That's because you were gawking at lover boy over there. I always wondered why you kicked me to the curb, but now I see it's because you never got over Sampson." His whisky breath poured over her making her nearly gag.

Years ago—when she'd dated him—she had thought he was an attractive man, with his blond hair and chocolate-colored eyes. He had a runner's body, lean and strong, he was about her height and he'd been fun to go out with for a while. Maybe he still was attractive to some people, but his personality was so nasty, and he'd been such a jerk when she broke it off, that she couldn't see past his actions to his looks any longer.

"Aaron no... how do you even know about Steve?"

"People talk Patricia and I have eyes; I can see the way you look at him. But the writing is on the wall, he'll just dump you again and if you come running back to me, this time I'll expect more than your wimpy platonic relationship."

"Well, you can count on me *not* coming back to you or your demands." She started to walk past him.

He grabbed her arm and leaned into her face. His breath washed over her in a stench of booze. "We'll see about that, woman."

She grit her teeth and spoke low. "Let go of me right now. Stop acting like a jerk. This is not the place for that behavior, Aaron."

"I don't give a damn where we are, you used me for weeks to take you out, always keeping me at arm's length, you're just a tease. Well, one of these days I'm going to collect on what you owe me."

"I don't owe you anything."

He shook her, before he released her arm. "That's what *you* think, missy."

"You need to leave now. You're making a scene that we don't need at this event."

"Fine, but this isn't over." He stalked away taking the stairs two at a time.

She rubbed her arm where he had clutched it, she was going to have bruises tomorrow from the jerk.

She turned to continue on her circuit of the room and Steve stepped up to her.

"Who was that harassing you?"

She shrugged. "Just some guy I dated, a long time ago, he's on the coaching staff. Coaches track and cross country."

"I got over here as quick as I could, without making a scene, what was he saying to you."

"Nothing of importance."

"Patsy…"

"No Steve, drop it, he's not worth our time or effort. I'm

not even sure why he was here tonight, he's not an engineer, probably for the free booze. Although, how he got in without a badge I don't know." She rubbed her arm again and then wished she hadn't when it caught Steve's attention.

"He hurt you."

"No, well, a little, just squeezed my arm, it'll be fine."

He took her hand and led her over by the bathrooms where there were a lot less people. He stopped with his back to the room to shield her from view, and pushed the sleeve up on her arm. There was an angry red mark from his hand, every finger clearly visible.

"Asshole, I should go pound on him. I hate men who manhandle a woman. You're going to have a bruise tomorrow. Maybe we should put some ice on it."

"Steve stop, it's fine, yes I'll probably have a bruise, but try not to go all crazy on me. I've gotten hurt worse rock hounding."

"But this was deliberate—"

She smiled at him and patted his hand. "I'm okay, it's not a big deal, let's go back to the party now. I don't think I've drank half of my lemonade, yet."

"No and it's probably hot and nasty by now, you go sit with Jamal and I'll get you a new one."

She nodded, relieved that he was calming down. It was nice he wanted to protect her and make sure she was alright, but she didn't need him to make a big deal of it.

STEVE WALKED OFF TO GET PATSY A NEW DRINK AND TO CALM down, he was so furious. When he had seen that jerk manhandling Patsy, he'd seen red and wanted to pummel the little toad. He knew she didn't want a scene at her party, so he had to calm down. He walked over to the bar and asked for a beer and a hard lemonade. He put a nice tip into the tip jar and turned around to find Ramona behind him. He groaned inwardly, not again.

"I know Ramona, I'm not going to hurt her."

She blinked at him. "What? Oh, no, I came over to find out what that asshole, Aaron Silverton, was harassing Patricia about."

Aaron Silverton, now he knew the name of the prick, thanks to Ramona. "She wouldn't tell me, said it wasn't important. Do you have any idea?"

"I'm guessing he was harassing her about not sleeping with him. They dated for a while shortly after you got married, kind of a rebound guy, I think. When she wouldn't sleep with him, he got kind of nasty and she broke it off. It's been years since she's gone out with him, so I don't know why he would be harassing her now. I don't like men who think they can push a woman around."

He remembered Patsy had said Ramona had been in an abusive marriage. No wonder she had come to ask him about Silverton. He didn't want to let on that Patsy had said anything about it, so he shrugged. "She thought he was drunk. Some people are jerks when they drink."

"True, and from my knowledge he was an asshole, even when he was not drunk. Thanks for watching out for her."

"She means a lot to me Ramona."

Ramona nodded. "I'm sure she does, and I really hope you show it better this time around."

"I will. I promise."

CHAPTER 17

*H*ours later Patricia groaned as she took off her shoes and left them by the door. She hobbled over to the couch and flopped down on it. "Oh my God, I'm glad to have those damn shoes off. Why, just tell me why, cute shoes always have to be uncomfortable. You try them on in the store and they are so cute, not terribly comfortable, but not killers either, so you buy them and then they become torture devices from hell. Hell, I tell you."

Steve chuckled and sat down next to her on the couch, drawing her feet into his lap where he inspected her right foot. "They were very cute, but look at where the straps were, they've rubbed your foot red. I don't think it's a good sign that I can see exactly where the straps sat." He lifted her right foot and kissed where the straps had been. "Poor baby foot."

Each touch of his lips sent a rush of tingles up her body as he softly kissed every strap mark. He put her foot back down into his lap and she wished there had been more straps on the implements of torture masquerading as shoes. But he started massaging that foot from toes to heel. She felt him rub out each ache, each pain and she decided he was welcome to stay and give her foot massages for the rest of her life. He gave a great foot massage.

He finished with the right foot and she wanted to cry, but then he started on the left one— and she actually purred —when he lifted that foot to his mouth to kiss the strap marks on it. It was the most erotic feeling ever, to have him kissing and massaging away the discomfort of the evening spent on her feet, while keeping the reception running smoothly.

When he had both of her feet singing happy songs, she struggled to rouse herself out of the euphoria he had put her in. "Okay, you're hired, you're now my official foot masseuse."

"Oh, and what do you plan to pay me with," he murmured.

She looked at him and saw lust in his eyes, she gently nudged her foot next to his groin and felt the evidence that he had worked himself into a completely different state than euphoria. She rubbed her foot along his length, he growled. She smiled and rubbed it again with a firmer touch.

"You're asking for it, woman."

"Yes Steve, yes, I am, asking for it. Let's go upstairs and get comfortable, or at least naked."

He lifted her feet and scooted around them, placing one arm under her knees and the other behind her back, he easily lifted her and carried her out of the room. She wrapped her arms around his neck and snuggled into his chest. He smelled delicious, just a hint of aftershave and another hint of beer, and the rest was all man; specifically, Steve, her man, at least for today.

She decided right then and there, she was going all in tonight, no more holding back in fear, no more keeping her heart and body locked in a box to keep it from getting bruised. She wasn't going to have him forever, but she was going to relish every second they did have.

Damned if she was going to look back in a week or two and wish she'd let herself enjoy it more. Nope all in, she'd deal with the loneliness and heart break of him leaving when he was gone. No sense in depriving herself of his presence in preparation for his leaving. That was just fool-ishness.

He took the stairs two at a time and was up to his room in seconds. He laid her gently on the bed and stepped back, just looking at her.

"What?"

"Nothing, just admiring the view. I like seeing you all soft and relaxed with your hair on my pillow."

She rolled her eyes at him. "Silly man."

"Not silly at all, I've always loved looking at you, God how I missed it the last ten years. I'm not sure I want to go back to that."

She sat up and placed her hand on his lips. "Shhh don't talk about that now, let's just enjoy each other and the time we do have. I plan to revel in you, and I expect you to revel in me. We've got this minute, this hour, this day, let's not waste it with thoughts of another day, another time. I want you to make love to me Steve, not just sex but the whole enchilada, let's see if we can't make this a night we remember our whole lives."

He grinned under her hand. "I can do that."

"Good, now let's get this foxy outfit off of you, shall we? I don't think I mentioned how sexy you looked all dressed up tonight. I wasn't sure I could keep my hands off of you during the reception, which is why I kept busy running around." She pulled the blue tie loose and worked the end out so the knot would unravel. Then she pushed his navy suit coat off his broad shoulders, running her hands up his chest and down his arms with the coat.

She reached for his belt and heard him suck in a breath, when she "accidentally" brushed the front of his slacks. Taking her sweet time, she slowly undid the button at the top and pulled the zipper down, making sure her hand caressed him through the slacks the whole time.

Steve grabbed her hand. "Enough of that little miss tease, your turn." He took her by the shoulders and turned her around while running his hands down her arms. Then he caressed her butt and ran his hands up her back, to ease the zipper down one click at a time. When it was fully unzipped, he stroked her bare back and flipped open the clasp on her bra, and pushed her dress down her body by smoothing his hands down the front of her. He lightly grazed her breasts, and she hissed in a breath, wanting him to touch her harder. But he didn't, he just moved in closer from behind and rubbed his erection against her back.

She tried to turn, but he held her still, by caressing her breasts and tweaking the nipples lightly, causing them to furl into tight buds. He kissed her shoulder and up her neck to her left ear where he licked the lobe. She squirmed and he ran his right hand down the front of her, where she was sure he could feel her arousal from her wet panties. He cupped her and pulled her back more firmly against him.

"Steve," she said on a moan.

"Yes darling, we can take care of you right now." He turned her so she was facing the bed. "Put your hands on the bed now and don't move."

She leaned forward and put her hands on the bed. He pushed her panties and hose down her legs and helped her step out of them. On his way back up he kissed the very top cleft of her ass and pushed her legs further apart with his feet.

His slacks hit the floor in a whoosh, and she heard him tear open a packet from the nightstand.

His penis caressed her from behind, slipping in the moisture from her body, rubbing from front to back and then returning to do it again and again. She wriggled, but he held her still and then eased himself inside her from behind, it was so different than anything she had ever felt before. The angle was changed, and it hit new spots in her body, igniting her passions. He rocked fully into her, she moaned and gripped the covers on the bed.

He held her hips still and pumped into her, over and over and she felt the storm gathering in a way it never had before. He reached around with one hand and pinched her clit just once. She went off like a roman candle, as wave after wave of pleasure crashed through her body. She screamed his name and felt her inner muscles clench down on him. He shouted her name in return, and she milked him.

They both collapsed on the bed side by side. He pulled the condom off and leaned up enough to drop it in the trash can that was now beside his nightstand. Then he turned her and pulled her up, so she was more fully on the bed, pulled the blankets over them and relaxed next to her. She snuggled over closer to him and he put his arms around her, she laid her head on his chest and they drifted.

STEVE WAS COMPLETELY CONTENT HOLDING PATSY IN HIS arms, he kissed the top of her head and breathed in the scent of her hair, so fresh with a slight floral and citrusy smell. She slowly raised her face toward his. He kissed her forehead and the tip of her nose, until his mouth settled on hers in a long drugging kiss.

When he lifted his lips from hers, he said, "I hope I wasn't too rough on you."

She smiled at him, looking radiant and so damn beautiful. "Not at all, it was a unique experience for me, but it was awesome, it felt so different."

He kissed her nose again. "None of your other lovers took you from behind? Stupid men, missed the boat."

She ducked her head and kissed his shoulder.

"Patsy? What is it?"

"Nothing important."

He took her chin in his hand and raised it, so he was looking into her eyes. "Tell me."

She squirmed and tried to look away, but he held her firmly. Finally, she took a big breath and said softly, "You're my one and only lover, Steve."

He felt that statement like a punch to the stomach. Her only lover, in ten years? She'd never had another? How was that possible? He knew he was her first, but she was a sensual woman who enjoyed sex. How could that be true?

"I don't understand, you like sex."

"I do, but I never felt like I wanted to have relations with anyone I dated." She shrugged and twirled her finger in his chest hair.

He sighed. "I really did a number on you, leaving, didn't I?"

"No, it's not that Steve, I wasn't afraid to try again, and I went out with several guys, but when it got close to heading to the bedroom, I just didn't care for them enough, so I broke it off. Which is what Aaron was bitching about earlier. He felt like I led him on and then never paid up."

"What an ass. It's your body and you're not obligated to share it with anyone you don't want to, regardless of the length of the relationship or the amount of time and money spent. The guy is a dick of the first order."

She kissed his neck and snuggled in closer. "I don't want to talk about him. But thanks. We should probably get some sleep; you have to go and be charming tomorrow. It's a tough job, but somebody has to do it."

He laughed and tickled her ribs. "Charming huh? Well I can try, I suppose."

"Shouldn't be too hard, just flash those baby blues and pearly whites and you're good to go."

He muttered, "Sleep, you need sleep, you're getting delirious."

She snuggled into him and he put his chin on the top of her head. He forced his body to relax while his mind churned, he could feel her body softening, relaxing and he willed her to sleep.

What an incredibly selfish bastard he'd been ten years ago, thinking he was being all self-sacrificing, helping Katerina and Thomas and leaving behind his sweetheart, Patsy. He'd convinced himself he'd been the only one hurt by his decisions. But now he saw things differently, he'd tossed away something precious, with hardly a thought.

He even began to wonder how much of his broken marriage had been his own fault. Had he treated Katerina, like she'd been a burden to him? He had never believed so before, but now he wondered. Had he treated her like she wasn't as good as Patsy, it's possible.

Did he compare the two and found Katerina wanting? Maybe he had, he couldn't remember ever rubbing the soreness out of Katerina's feet or fussing over her. He hadn't treated her bad, but he hadn't treated her special either.

What an ass he was, well his eyes were opened now, and he wasn't going to remain an ass. Time to grow up and quit being the martyr. He didn't know exactly how to accomplish that, but he was going to try to remain alert to his selfish behavior.

He held a precious bundle in his arms, and he was, by God, going to become a man worthy of her love and affection.

CHAPTER 18

*S*teve groaned at the thought of getting up, but he had to, the summit started today. He let his eyes just barely slit open and he saw bright sunlight, streaming in through the window. Damn, he needed to get up, the opening session was set up to start at eleven, so he had plenty of time, but still he needed to get moving.

He let his eyes drift shut blocking out the sunlight and wondered where Patsy was. He was still a little freaked out about her confession last night and his own realizations.

On one hand, he was honored that she had shared her body with him and only him. But on the other hand, he was embarrassed that he had thought nothing of leaving her, thinking she would bounce back into a new relationship.

There wasn't anything to do about it now, except learn from it. What he was supposed to learn and how he was supposed to change—now that was the question.

He deliberately turned his mind to the conference. The focus of the first meeting this morning was on the different experts who had come in to share their knowledge, each one was being given a ten-minute time period, to give the highlights of what they planned to focus on during the week.

He would be giving several workshops, and then his keynote speech was on Friday night to wrap up the summit. There were several other experts that were holding workshops also.

His specialty was mine reclamation, how to clean it up after the fact and maybe more importantly how to avoid having to do too much cleanup, with careful planning before mining began. There were a lot of different mining operations in Virginia and West Virginia. Gold, coal, uranium, and gems, were all found between the two states, so he had a lot of experience seeing the best and the worst of practices. He was experimenting with microbes for smaller mines that didn't warrant a million-dollar water treatment plant, but still needed to be cleaned up to not contaminate nearby water supplies.

What they knew now, compared to how mining operations had been done in the past, was similar to medicine, back when they used to bleed people to try to get the impurities out of the blood, to modern day practices. Yeah, dark ages versus modern knowledge, we've come a long way, but the mining operations of the past were still causing problems today.

So, his job was to educate new mine owners, and at the same time find ways to clean up the environment from the past. His alma mater was one of the leading schools doing research. There were a lot of old mines in Colorado to work with. Over a thousand miles of waterways were affected by the drainage of the 23,000 old mine features in Colorado alone. It was easier to do research in a teaching environment rather than in the business sector. But he was making a difference and that's what mattered.

He glared at the sunlight and started to sit up when Patsy

came into his room, fully dressed, with a cup of coffee in her hands. "Oh, good you're awake. I guess you got, acclimated to our time zone."

He growled. "I think it's more a fact of you keeping me up half the night at the reception and then wearing me out with sex."

The smile she directed at him was huge. "Sex is a good way to get tired, nothing worth growling about. You're sounding a little cranky—but never fear—the coffee will help, and when you come down from your shower, I'll have a nice hot breakfast waiting for you."

"I would be less grumpy if you showered with me."

She backed up with her hands out. "Oh no, *I* am showered, dressed, my hair is done, and I even have makeup on. Not starting over. Now you just drink your coffee and come down when you're ready for gourmet breakfast." She practically skipped out of the room.

He took a big gulp of his coffee, set it on the nightstand and flopped back in bed hitting his head on the wrought iron headboard. Damn that hurt. Maybe it would knock some sense into him. He wondered if he should mention her revelation from last night, it had never in a million years crossed his mind, that she hadn't had other lovers, in the ten years they'd been apart. She was so beautiful and sensual, what in the hell was wrong with the guys here.

Well obviously, that one jerk had tried to get in her pants, Steve was damn glad she hadn't let *him*. Any man that felt a woman owed him sex, was a prick, that didn't deserve a special woman like Patsy. He might just have to look up his old coach while he was here and make sure the man knew what kind of asshole he had working for him. Coach Calhoun had not allowed any disrespect of women, when he oversaw the track team. He couldn't imagine him wanting that kind of man on his staff.

He better get his lazy ass out of this bed; the woman was cooking, and it didn't bode well for a man to let that kind of effort go to waste. He got out of bed and headed for the shower.

PATRICIA STARTED IN ON BREAKFAST. SHE WAS NERVOUS AND she had to stay busy. There were some ham cubes in the freezer, she got one baggie of them out, so they could start thawing. She whipped up some dough for biscuits and rolled them out, got out the cookie cutter and cut nice little circles, putting them on the cookie sheet. Gathering the remnants, she rolled them out again to cut more and then put the cookie sheet in the oven to bake.

She hoped Steve wouldn't bring up her admission from last night. Whatever had possessed her to tell him anyway? How pathetic did that make her look; it wasn't like she'd been pining for him the whole time. She just hadn't liked anyone well enough to have sex with them.

She got the green onions and a red bell pepper out and started chopping them into small pieces. But no, she could jump Steve again, just barely thirty hours after he'd come into town. So, she went from the ice princess, that she was certain some of the faculty called her, to a ho in less than two days.

She dumped the veggies and ham cubes into the skillet to brown just a bit. Was it her fault none of those other guys she'd dated did anything for her? There hadn't been any sexual attraction to them. She'd enjoyed hanging out with them, going to dinner or movies or concerts, but sex? No, she just wasn't interested.

There were oranges in the fridge, she got some out and cut them in half to squeeze to make orange juice. She'd wondered if Steve had broken something inside her and she would never feel aroused again. Nope the man didn't have to do anything, but be in the room, and she was aroused.

That just didn't seem fair. Most of those other guys had been perfectly nice men who she laughed and had fun with, but there had been no spark. She got the eggs out and whipped four of them together and dumped them in the skillet along with some frozen hash browns. Aaron was one of two that had tried to force the issue. The other one had thought she was playing hard to get or some kind of dominance game, but once she'd made it clear that was not the case, he'd backed right down and they were friendly when they bumped into each other.

She stirred the eggs and put honey and butter on the table with plates, glasses and utensils. Aaron was the only one that was still hostile, and it wasn't just because Steve was in town. Snide remarks and vicious gossip seemed to be Aaron's forte, he'd started in right after she broke up with him, but she'd learned to ignore it and none of the guys on campus seemed to give his comments credence anymore.

She heard the water turn off in the shower, so she put the biscuits in a basket with a cloth napkin around them to hold in the heat. Then put some cheese in the eggs and decided to set out some jam too, in case Steve preferred it. He walked in looking all sexy with his hair a little damp. Nope, nothing at all wrong with her girl parts, at least where *this* man was concerned. She scooped the eggs onto the pretty blue plates, as he refilled his coffee cup.

"Wow, you weren't kidding about gourmet breakfast, look at this egg scramble, homemade biscuits, and fresh squeezed orange juice. It looks and smells awesome."

She grinned and curtsied, pretending to hold out a dress.

He laughed and pulled her in for a nice long kiss. She melted into him for just a few moments before she pushed him back. "Now don't you go starting anything Steve Sampson and ruin my hard work by letting it get all cold and nasty."

"Yes ma'am." He sat and grabbed a couple of biscuits out of the basket. Patsy watched in awe, as he slathered them with half a cube of butter and then drowned them in honey.

"Steve, some of your calories for the day should come from protein, not just carbs."

He grinned at her and shoved half of a biscuit in his mouth. His eyes nearly rolled back in his head, and she decided he must be enjoying it. She shook her head and buttered her biscuit with far less butter and just a little honey.

He finished chewing. "I haven't had home-made biscuits in so long I can't remember when. They are delicious, ambrosia of the gods."

She rolled her eyes. "I don't know how you even tasted them smothered in butter and honey."

"I have very discriminating taste buds. I could taste them just fine, and they are amazing."

"Uh huh, eat your eggs."

"Happy to, so anything I need to know for this morning's meeting?" He forked up a large bite of eggs and crammed his mouth full. What was it with guys that they still ate like little kids?

"Not really, everyone will give their mini speech on what they plan to share in depth during their workshops. It gives the attendees the ability to determine who they want to listen to, some of the workshops overlap so we want to help people select easier."

She shrugged and continued, "We're trying to have only

two experts per hour with some professors and research people in the mix to give everyone a chance to attend workshops, even you. Most of the talks will be recorded for people to listen to the ones they didn't attend, when they get home." She took a bite of her biscuit and decided they were good, of course she could *actually* taste hers.

He raised an eyebrow. "Are you giving any workshops?"

"Yes, two, one on some fossils we found, on a field trip, that might be indicative of fossil fuel in a previously ignored area. The second will be on the research that caused me to suggest we dig in the area we did yesterday."

He stopped with a forkful of eggs halfway to his mouth. "I hope my workshops are not at the same time as yours. I would like to hear both of them." He put the bite in his mouth and chewed.

She shook her head. "I'm sure you can find more interesting people to listen to."

"Patsy there is no one, on this planet, more interesting. I would really like to hear your talks." He took her hand and rubbed her knuckles. "Well unless you would give me a personal tutoring session."

She shivered at his touch and the look in his eyes. Now was not the time for desire.

"I don't think we're scheduled at the same time." She drew her hand back and made a big show of buttering another biscuit, even though she had half of one left on her plate. "There is a lunch after the opening session in the cafeteria, it's a little later than when the students eat, which is part of the reason I made us a big breakfast." She took a bite of the scramble and waved her fork at him to get eating.

He sighed dramatically, took a big drink of orange juice, and picked up his fork.

Dear God, the man made drinking orange juice sexy. She

watched as his throat worked to swallow and wanted to bite him or maybe lick his throat like an ice-cream cone, a warm ice-cream cone.

This was getting ridiculous, she didn't want him to notice her gawking, she looked away and squirmed in her chair a little. When she looked back at him, he was staring at her, she grinned at him and took another bite of the biscuit. At least she wasn't the only one.

CHAPTER 19

*J*amal opened the summit, welcoming all the people present and introducing the various experts, who had come in to share their knowledge with the attendees assembled in the auditorium. Jamal had a stirring speech about the need to protect the environment while at the same time providing the world with the energy it needed. There were experts on alternative fuel, new methods of extraction for minerals, oil and gas, and cleaning up the previously contaminated environment.

Steve was sitting next to Jamal, and he looked so damn good, all dressed up and professional. She hardly noticed the other people as they were introduced, but when it was Steve's turn, she was all ears.

His deep voice poured over her like warm chocolate, and when he spoke in his quiet, authoritative way she thought she might melt right there. She had never heard him speak professionally and it was a sight to behold. His confidence and expertise was so appealing; she just knew everyone in the room had to be hanging on every word. Plus, his subject was so new and unique it was bound to be a successful topic.

She quickly glanced around, and it did appear that he held the attention of every person in the room. When he finished his short speech, she wanted to beg him to continue, just so she could keep listening to his deep voice. She shook herself out of the stupor his few minutes had put her in, his workshops were going to be packed, and she was going to be right in there with the rest of the crowd. She hoped he was scheduled for a large room.

Jamal closed the opening meeting by introducing the committee, so people knew who could answer questions. He pointed out and explained where things were, including lunch, and dismissed everyone. Patsy was standing to the right of the room, so she could be seen by the attendees, but not be too obvious, she was more of a back-stage kind of committee member, they had plenty that liked to be front and center. She was perfectly capable of being *on stage,* but she didn't need it to be fulfilled.

She noticed Steve moving in her direction, but he was stopped often as people tried to engage him to talk about his subject more. He didn't encourage any of them to linger, but he smiled and was warm to them, while steadily making his way toward her. She answered a few questions and pulled out the conference program, to check which rooms Steve was scheduled to present in. She was relieved to see he was assigned one of the larger auditoriums for each one of his workshops, at least they didn't need to scramble to get him into a large room.

He finally appeared before her and took her arm to draw her close. He whispered, "I need a shield, these people are rabid to find out about the microbes. I'm going to explain everything in detail in the workshops."

She whispered back, "I'll handle it." She turned to the people trailing after him. "Folks please head directly to the cafeteria, I'm sure we have enough food for everyone, but we wouldn't want anyone to miss out on their lunch. Mr. Sampson will be here all week, so there will be plenty of time for you to ask him any questions he doesn't cover in the workshops. Right now, he's committed to a quick meeting."

The people muttered but split off to go to the luncheon. Steve sighed in relief when the last one left. "I didn't expect to be mugged. I know it's an interesting topic, but still."

She laughed. "Charming, you're supposed to be charming."

He frowned at her. "I don't think I need to be, in fact, I might need some mace or something to keep them back."

"Right, let's go eat."

"What time is the next workshop? How much time is set aside for lunch?"

"About two hours. We wanted to make sure everyone had time to get to the cafeteria, be served, eat and check email or anything else they needed to do, and be back in time and settled for the workshops."

"Perfect." He took her hand and started pulling her to the back of the building.

She stopped. "Steve, the cafeteria—"

"Yes, I know but I don't want cafeteria food, I don't want cafeteria company, I don't want to see the cafeteria."

"Well, what do you want to eat, see and talk to then?"

"You."

She squeaked, "Me?"

He nodded. "You, now, at your house. Any objections?"

"Other than you're the keynote and you're supposed to be mingling and being charming."

"Only one person I want to charm and that's you, out of your clothes."

"But…" She vaguely waived toward the cafeteria.

"They won't even notice we're not there and you told a bunch of them I was going to be in a meeting. So, I will be… in a meeting… a very private meeting… for two."

She couldn't deny to him or herself, it sounded like a great idea.

STEVE WAS THRILLED WHEN PATSY DIDN'T ARGUE BUT LET him pull her along. He wanted to go eat with all those people like he wanted a hole in the head, and in the cafeteria, eating cafeteria food… no thank you. He would much rather get Patsy naked, or even if she didn't want to get naked, he would much rather talk to Patsy and eat her food, even just sandwiches or the left-over biscuits.

There were a lot of left-over biscuits, they could warm them up in the microwave and slather butter and honey on them. His mouth watered at the thought. Since they'd driven down, he steered her toward his rental car, it would be faster. He didn't want to rush once they got to her house.

When they got into his car, he turned to look at her. "You know, it's not just sex, right?" He rubbed his hand around the back of his neck. "I mean I would be happy to take you out to lunch, if there's somewhere you want to go. Or we can go back to your house and clean the rest of our collection of crystals.

"I just am not a big fan of the cafeteria's food, and I don't want to spend the whole time telling everyone individually, exactly what I'm going to say in the workshops. And well I just want to spend the time with you. Alone doing pretty much anything, eating whatever, even left-over biscuits."

A slow smile spread across her face and her eyes

sparkled. "So, you're saying you are at my disposal to do whatever I desire?"

"Sure, as long as it doesn't take over two hours, I have my first workshop after lunch. I don't really have anything I need to do to prepare for it other than showing up. I've got the handouts in the trunk."

"Hmm, well let me think. The house needs to be painted, but that would take longer than two hours, and I haven't quite decided on the final color. I need to plant some flowers in the beds out front, but they need to be weeded first and the ground prepared and that would also take longer than two hours."

Patsy put her hands on her hips. "I've been thinking about putting in a new sink in the guest bathroom, but I don't have the sink purchased yet and that would take longer than two hours. The picket fence could use a fresh coat of paint, but that takes a while too, and again I don't have the paint."

Her eyes lit up and she touched his arm. "I've been dying to try a new restaurant in Boulder, they serve high tea, and it looks like it would be so much fun to go, but that would take longer than two hours too." She shook her head sadly.

She tapped a finger to her lips and lust shot through him. Down boy, the woman had home repairs on her mind, and he was going to stand by his offer, even if it killed him. "Nope I can't think of anything we could do in less than two hours, so I guess we'll just have to have sex and eat left over biscuits."

"What?"

"Gotcha." She laughed like a loon at his confusion. "You should have seen your face, trying to be all stoic and helpful, when I listed all those home repairs, and even a frou-frou restaurant in Boulder. You would have gone even if it killed you. Which is all very sweet, but I'm not interested in any of that. Take me home, big boy, and ravish me."

Fire shot straight to his groin and he wasn't sure he was safe to drive, with the lack of blood in his brain right now, but he wasn't about to turn her down. He started the car and aimed it toward her house, glad it was only a few blocks. Especially when she reached over and put her hand in his lap.

She caressed him through his slacks, and he thought he might crash the car, from the lust and desire coursing through his body. The woman was asking for it, and he was just the man to deliver.

He pulled up in front of the house and she jumped out of it and raced into the front door. He turned off the car, shook his head and leaped out to follow her. Clearly, she was feeling frisky and he wasn't going to waste one second. When he got inside the door, he found a shoe and then a little further in another shoe, after that was the jacket she'd had on from her pantsuit, and then the belt.

He continued to follow the trail of clothes and started dropping his right along with hers. When he finally found her panties on the newel post at the top of the stairs, he dropped the rest of his clothes and made a quick detour to his room to grab condoms. Her door was open in invitation, so he thought she would be in there.

He walked into her bedroom and realized it was the first time he'd been in there. He hadn't noticed they'd had all their amorous encounters in his room, or the kitchen. He didn't see Patsy at first, so he looked around the room at her turquoise jewel box of a room. It was lavishly decorated in turquoise with white, pink and navy accents. She still had rocks everywhere and more pictures of her family.

She came out of the bathroom and smiled at him. "Good for you. I hoped you would take the hint and get naked too."

"Well with a trail of clothes to follow it wasn't hard to

figure out, and I didn't want to ruin the mood by being over-dressed."

"Excellent." She turned her back to him and bent over to pull the quilt down on her bed, giving him a delicious view of her very fine ass. He wanted to bite it. She looked over her shoulder and wiggled it at him. Now, he wanted to spank it.

He pounced on her and tossed her onto the bed. "Stop that, you bad girl."

She giggled and pinched his nipple. "Make me."

He started to move, and she reared up and slapped her hands on his shoulders to get him to lay down. "No wait, it's my turn. Lay down and keep still. No moving, no touching. It's my turn, to play with your body."

He grinned at her and spread his arms wide. "Be my guest."

She rubbed her hands together and licked her lips, as she looked him over from head to toe. She let her gaze slowly caress him and when she looked at his groin his cock jumped in anticipation. She leered at him, and then spoke to his cock as she softly stroked it, "Now don't you worry, I won't ignore you." It jumped in her hand and that made her laugh. "But you're going to have to wait and be patient, because there's a big, beautiful man here, and his whole body deserves atten-tion, don't you think?"

Steve groaned as she started in on his body, touching and tasting, nipping, and licking every inch of him from his toes to his neck, except for his most sensitive area. She tormented him with pleasure but made his cock wait just as she'd said. He was gripping the sheets like a madman when she finally got to his face and kissed it all over.

Then she nipped his earlobe and whispered, "He's been very patient, so now I must reward him." She kissed her way down his chest until she got back to his cock. She kissed the very tip, and Steve used every bit of his willpower to stay still and let her play. But she was about to drive him right out of his ever-loving mind.

She caressed his balls with one hand and took the base of his cock in the other, then drew the tip into her warm hot mouth. Steve knew he'd just died and gone to heaven as she licked and sucked. She ran her tongue over and around, up and down. She used her hands just as skillfully, and Steve was certain he would just evaporate, from the sheer pleasure she was giving him.

When his body started gathering for release, he groaned her name. "Patsy, babe, stop I want to be inside you when I come."

She looked up at him and he could see her debating, then she reached over to the nightstand, grabbed a packet and tore it open. She slowly and with great care rolled it on him, and he wasn't sure he could stand anymore of her ministrations.

He groaned. "Babe…"

She crawled up his body, letting her breasts caress him, until they were in his face and he snatched one into his mouth, as she lined herself up with him and slid down. He released her nipple, so she could fully seat herself on him.

She looked at him. "You are allowed to move and touch me now."

She gasped as he whipped her over underneath him and started pounding into her, he couldn't help himself, he'd exerted every bit of control he had to not move, and there was nothing left to hold himself back. So, he let her have every-thing that was in him. His mouth latched onto hers and the kiss was as furious as his body. But she met him stroke for stroke with her tongue and her pelvis, as she wrapped her legs around his waist, and her arms around his shoulder. They rode like warriors into the heat, into the flames, and exploded together in a volcanic explosion, that mimicked Mount Saint Helens.

When his heart had slowed to the point that it wasn't thundering in his ears, he rolled off of Patsy, and lay next to her on her bed. She was staring at the ceiling, not really moving much. "I'm, um, did I hurt you, I kind of lost control there."

She slowly turned her head toward him, and a smile so large, so luminous, was on her face that he felt himself relax. "Hurt? No not at all, and I absolutely love that I made you lose control."

"What?"

"Oh yeah, that was awesome, you've been a very kind and considerate lover, but I always felt out of control, and you seemed to be just the opposite. But this time I was in control, and you lost it completely, and I loooooove that, Steve, I truly love it."

"Oh, well, good I guess. Glad I could make you happy by going all cave man on you."

She giggled and he felt his heart settle. "By all means Steve, cave man away."

He reached over and yanked on a lock of her hair. "Don't tempt me woman, you might just get more than you are looking for."

"Oh, no, I don't think so, Steve. I'm looking for whatever you've got. She glanced past him and frowned. "We probably need to get moving, we have to get dressed and have a bite to eat, and we've only got forty-five minutes left of our lunch break."

He pulled her close and kissed her thoroughly, not really wanting to let her go. But they didn't have any choice, they had commitments and time stopped for no man, or woman.

CHAPTER 20

*a*s each day of the summit passed, Patricia felt herself becoming more frantic, more obsessed with spending every minute possible with Steve. She went to his workshops, she went to the workshops he was going to sit in on, she went to find him after she had to go do something for the summit committee. She started resenting the committee obligations, that at one time she had been excited about. She was becoming a maniac, or maybe just crazy.

No, she knew deep down what she was doing, what she was doing was trying to cram a lifetime of love and together-ness into a week. It was pitiful and stupid, but she just couldn't help herself. She went to the bare minimum amount of social obligations she could, as a member of the commit-tee. She and Steve would go in, show face, spend a few minutes chatting and then sneak out the door. Steve seemed perfectly happy to skip out on everything also. They spent all their free time at her house, talking, eating, but mostly making love.

They did manage to finish cleaning up the rest of the rock

samples they had collected, and Steve had taken his half, leaving her with plenty to display in her house and take to her classes. There was one particularly beautiful crystal structure that they decided to donate to the Geology Museum. It was so flawless and beautiful intact, that they didn't have the heart to chop it up into stones to be used in jewelry. It being at the museum, donated in their names, would keep it special and safe forever. It seemed kind of symbolic to have a piece of them and their lives put aside for posterity, especially since they would not have a lifetime together.

Patricia had to admit she had given the idea of moving back with him some thought. But he didn't live near any school where she could continue her teaching, and she just didn't have it in her to go into the corporate sector, even doing something like Steve was doing, in mine planning and reclamation. Teaching had become her first love, watching the students learn about how the earth was formed, watching them become curious and interested in discovery. And she loved being able to take her students out to the field, to guide them into knowledge, to help them see right before their eyes, what had happened hundreds of thousands of years before.

She'd looked up online what was around his area, to see if she could find something, anything, and had fallen flat. It had made her sad, but she'd worked hard to put that sadness behind her and focus on the moment. Because if the moment was all they were going to have, she damn well was not going to waste it being sad. She could be sad later, right now she had the man she loved in her home and in her bed, and she was going to revel in each and every moment.

Their love making became more frantic as each day passed, they hardly made it in the door before clothes started flying. Hungry mouths and desperate hands fought for purchase, fought for sensation, fought for anything. Every last sensation was savored, every touch, every taste, every scent. She watched him as their passions rose, memorizing each look, each expression. She wished she could record it all, to watch, again and again, in the months and years to come.

That time loomed ahead of her and it felt stark and lonely.

HOW COULD THE DAYS BE FLYING BY SO FAST? STEVE couldn't believe it was nearly time to leave this place, the summit was almost over. A week had seemed like plenty of time to find closure with Patsy. He'd thought they could make love and then move on with their lives, but as the time got shorter, he felt desperate to change something. He didn't want to leave, he wanted to stay right here with Patsy. He searched his brain for a way to stay, but every idea had an impelling reason why it wouldn't work.

He just couldn't justify leaving his family high and dry. What if his dad got up on a ladder to fix the roof and fell off? What if little Kevin needed a man to guide him when he got in school? What if there was a bully and he needed to learn to defend himself? Kevin was only four and had years and years of potential trouble ahead. Yes, maybe he was being overprotective and over committed, but it's who he was, fundamentally. He could no more change his personality than fly to the moon.

And there was nothing in his vicinity that Patsy would enjoy working at, he was smack dab in a concrete jungle with no colleges that had any kind of mineral engineering. It was one of the reasons he had come to Colorado for his education. Oh, there were colleges within commuting distance, so if she was an IT professor, she had all kinds of choices, or medical or law, or hell, even literature and fine arts, but not any of the mineral sciences, and certainly not geology. And there wasn't anywhere for her to go and get away for exploring, at least not for a day trip. She would shrivel up and die. Ten years ago, things might have been different, they could have gone into environmental engineering together, but now, he just couldn't see it.

He wanted to ask her, beg her to try, but he loved her too much to hurt her like that. Either she would say yes and leave the profession she loved and slowly die inside. Or she would tell him no and feel guilty about it. So, he had no intention of asking her. And that depressed the hell out of him, but he was bound and determined not to let it show. He would not taint his last few hours with the woman he loved, by being depressed. No way, no how.

Instead, he poured his love for her into every kiss, every smile, every touch. He sensed she was doing the same thing. What a pair they were, like star crossed lovers. Still, he thought about trying to have a long-distance relationship, visiting each other as often as possible, and he had every intention of working on that. Planning to email and call and facetime frequently. And be on every plane heading this direction that he could manage.

Maybe he could get on a committee of professionals that were helping with the mine reclamation research here on campus. Then he would have an even better excuse to come out more often, sometimes even on the company dime. He needed to talk to the faculty head doing the research and see if that was possible.

Because he just didn't think he had it in him to walk away from her completely. It had been a long ten years without her. He hadn't realized how much he missed her until he was back here. Thinking on the last ten years made him realize that his life seemed dark and a dull gray color.

The last week had been bright, like looking through a rainbow. He didn't want to go back to the dull and gray, he loved the rainbow. So even if he only had the rainbow for a few minutes on the phone, or a week every month or two, it was still better than the alternative.

CHAPTER 21

Steve felt his phone vibrate in his pocket, the workshop he was in was over, so he slipped out the back of the room and saw his sisters face. He pushed the talk button.

"Hey Sis, how's it going?"

"Awesome, are you busy? Can you talk? Am I calling at a bad time?"

"As a matter of fact, it's a perfect time, the workshop just ended, so I have fifteen minutes, or more if needed. I hadn't decided about the next set of workshops and I'm done speaking for today." He walked outside to sit on the wide banisters that surrounded the porch of the building.

"Yay, because I just had to call you to tell you my great news!"

"Well then tell me."

"Gabe is coming home!" she squealed.

"That's great sweetie, I'm sure Kevin will be thrilled to have his dad home for a while."

"No, not for a while, for good, he's been working toward a classification to keep him home. He's been keeping it quiet because he didn't want to get anyone's hopes up, in case he failed. But he didn't fail, he's going to be home for good. We'll have to move closer to West Point so he can finish his degree and then he'll start teaching. Isn't that awesome?"

"Oh, Theresa, sweetheart that's the best news ever. I'm so happy for you." He heard her sniff and knew she was crying.

"I'm happy for me too. I'll miss all of you, but I'm just so darn happy to have my man coming home for good."

"Don't you worry about that, we'll be coming to visit so often, you'll get sick and tired of us." He looked across the commons toward the admin building, it was a beautiful spring day.

She laughed a watery laugh. "I'm going to hold you to that Brother, little Kevin is going to miss his Uncle Steve."

"He'll have his dad to make up for it, and if I know Mom and Dad, they'll be camped out on your front porch."

She laughed. "Speaking of that, they got back from their cruise yesterday and they're talking about getting a trailer, and I quote, seeing America with lots of trips in my direction."

"Really, they always talked about doing that when we were kids, do you remember?"

"Yes, Mom had that road atlas that she used to pour over, all the time. I think I knew where each state was, before I knew the alphabet."

"Do you think they'll really do it?" he asked.

"There isn't much stopping them if I'm moving. Dad checked in with the business when they got back and they didn't need him, everything is running smoothly there. The house is paid off, they could sell it for a bundle, or rent it out, or even just let it sit there, for when they got tired of having a home on four wheels.

They admitted they've been out looking for trailers and

they considered the cruise a test run. They were looking even before they heard about Gabe and me moving. I think they didn't want to mention it in case I freaked out. You and Rebecca are much more independent, and with no families, you could always just fly in to wherever they were at the moment."

"True, that might actually be kind of fun. Fly into Florida for Christmas, or Oregon for Easter." He laughed. "What an adventure that would be."

"Yeah, I hope they actually do it, and don't waste their opportunity to live a dream they've had all their married lives. They're still young enough and able bodied."

"That's true and it would keep Dad from trying to fix the roof or trim the trees away from the electrical wires."

She chuckled. "Your own private nightmares."

"You got that right. When Mom calls and tells me, Dad's getting the ladder out, I break out in a cold sweat. I'll be back in a few days and we can see what they're thinking. I'm glad you called to tell me your news."

"Me too, now get to your next workshop. I didn't keep you too long."

"No, you didn't, love you."

"Love you too, Big Brother, see you in a few days."

Steve put the phone back in his pocket and stared across the commons. So, most of his family was going to be leaving Virginia, were they? He'd thought he was tied to the place because of his responsibilities to them, but if they weren't there, what would keep him from moving? His job and his older sister were both there. But he could get another job, and he hardly saw Rebecca, she was so busy with her career. He needed to think about this more. Maybe he didn't have to leave Patsy again.

His attention was attracted by a man who looked familiar

even from clear across the commons. Coach Calhoun, now that was someone he wanted to have a word with. He stood and took the steps at a quick pace and jogged across the grass.

Coach noticed him coming and stopped, a big smile spreading across his face. "Sampson, I heard you were the keynote for the summit this year. I hoped I would see you."

"I planned to come by the gym Coach but hadn't found the time yet." He was too busy seducing Patsy every free minute of the day.

"Not a coach anymore, getting to old to keep up with these kids. I'm the head of the department these days, sitting in my easy chair, letting the young guys manage the students."

"I did see that in the Alumni magazine, congrats on the promotion. But I still think you could run circles around them all." Steve shook his hand.

"Hit the double nickel last year and I have no desire to run circles around anyone. I keep in shape, but that's about it."

"So just kickin' back… I'll bet your 'keeping in shape' is on the order of a five K." Steve smiled making air quotes. Then he frowned. "I was wondering about one of your coaches."

"Oh, which one?"

"Aaron Silverton."

Coach Calhoun grimaced. "Not my favorite."

"Yeah, lets walk and talk, shall we." Steve was going to put a bug in his ear about the track and field instructor. Coach Calhoun ran a tight ship, and he wasn't going to like hearing what Steve had to say.

"I'm all ears."

PATRICIA ROUNDED THE CORNER AND SAW HER SORORITY sisters in an intense conversation. She thought about turning around and avoiding them, but Carol saw her, said something to the other girls and they all turned toward her putting their hands on their hips. Damn, they weren't happy. She squared her shoulders, plastered an innocent smile on her face, and walked toward them.

Before she even said a word, Ramona said, "Where have you been? We haven't seen you three times since we got here nearly a week ago."

Carol piped up, "Yeah, your conference duties can't keep you that busy."

Conference duties, excellent excuse. There was no way she was going to tell them she'd been spending every minute she had free, jumping in bed with Steve. "Oh girls, poor Jamal was so sick, he's still feeling a little weak. I've had to—"

Betsy shook her finger at her. "Now you just hold it right there, missy, we've seen a whole lot more of Jamal than we have of you. Poor, weak, Jamal is doing just fine, and if you were ever around you would know that. So, we aren't buying that BS for one minute."

Ramona and Carol were nodding right along with every word. Now what was she going to tell them. She really sucked at making up excuses on the fly. Fine, the truth it was. "I've been at home."

They just looked at her and waited. "With Steve."

Still, they just looked at her and waited. "Having sex."

Carol said, "Ha, told you, pay up," and held out a hand to both of the other girls.

Betsy ignored her. "Are you kidding me, after what you went through last time?"

Ramona said. "I knew we should have abducted her, the minute I heard he was going to be here."

Patricia laughed. "Now just hold on, this isn't like the last time. First, I was ten years younger. Second, I know what's going to happen this time, Steve is going back to his family in Virginia, and I'm staying here. Third, this is a no strings, getting it out of our systems kind of thing."

Betsy gasped. "Are you really that naïve, him leaving again is going to devastate you."

"No, it's not, I have no delusions this time." Patricia shook her head. "I know the score. I know how it's going to end. But I am damn well going to enjoy that man, while I have the chance."

They all three looked at her and then each other and Ramona shrugged. "Fine if you believe that, then we'll accept it. But when he leaves, we'll still be here for you."

"Thanks, but I'll be fine."

Carol patted her arm. "I hope so sweetie, I hope so."

Betsy reached in and grabbed her in a hug. "We love you, you know that, right?"

The other two joined the group hug. "I love you guys too," she said to her sisters, "But I'll be fine."

The girls walked off to head to the next workshop and Patsy kept the smile plastered on her face. She was going to be fine, wasn't she? She planned to be fine, she'd mostly talked herself into being fine. But would she really be fine, or was she just fooling herself? The thought of him leaving made her heart ache. She didn't think she could do a long distance, go visit each other relationship. Wouldn't that just mean having to say goodbye over and over again. Would a clean break be best, just a finite amount of pain and then move on? Sounded like the best idea to her, none of the lingering, wondering, hopefulness. Just cut the cord and move on.

But she wasn't fooling herself that it would be easy. She was going to miss his big warm body in bed. She was going to miss the companionship of cooking and eating together. She was going to miss him in her everyday life. It was going to suck, big time. Spring break was in a little over two weeks, maybe… no, cut the cord, move on. Yeah, move on.

So why did that idea hurt so bad?

CHAPTER 22

*S*teve was excited to have the summit nearly over. His speech last night had gone well. His bags were packed and in his rental car. The flight to take him back to Virginia was later tonight, so he had plenty of time, and he wanted to talk to Patsy about some of the decisions he'd made. But he wanted to wait until the summit was over, so he would have her full attention.

They were at the closing brunch, where each of the expert speakers were giving their last ten-minute speech. He'd already done his, so he was sitting at the table next to Patsy, enjoying the scent of her, drifting toward him. She was close enough, that their arms brushed when one of them reached for their coffee. He was going to doze on the plane, once it got in the air, they'd spent most of last night making love, and then again this morning. But he didn't mind, he could sleep later.

His mind drifted to all the things he would need to accomplish in the next few weeks to get his plans rolling in the right direction. He needed to talk to his folks to see if they were really going to be selling their home and taking off across America.

He'd called them yesterday and they had confirmed what Theresa had told him, and had expanded on what she'd said. They'd already put a down payment on the trailer and talked to a real estate agent about putting their house on the market. Apparently, they weren't even planning to wait until it sold, this was the best time to start on their adventure, with spring and summer right around the corner, and they'd decided to go big or go home. He'd laughed when his mother had told him that, he wasn't sure she even knew the reference to it.

He startled out of his musing when everyone started clapping. He clapped along with them and then they all started gathering up their possessions. Guess it was over. Anticipation soared in him, he'd probably have to wait while Patsy checked to make sure everything was moving according to plan. She might even have to help with the cleanup, but he could wait. He was so damn excited to tell her about his ideas that he felt like he might explode. But he was going to be patient and wait until he had her undivided attention, if it killed him.

He stood up and stretched, but someone caught his eye and he turned toward her. He couldn't believe what he was seeing he blinked and looked again. "Dammit, what's *she* doing here?"

Patsy looked at him and followed his gaze. "Who is that? She's beautiful."

"Yeah, I guess. That's my ex-wife, I'm going to go find out why she's here."

He stalked off across the room.

His ex-wife? Here in Colorado at the summit? That knowledge made Patricia's stomach knot in dread. He'd even agreed with her that she was beautiful. She watched as he approached her and took her wrist to lead her to the side of the room.

She watched in horror as Steve listened carefully to what his ex was saying, the more she talked the more engaged he became. Patricia could see tears on her face and saw her take both of his hands in hers. He nodded his head and turned it toward where Patricia was standing. Katerina pulled on him and he turned back to listen to what she had to say, and he nodded again. He turned toward Patricia and mimed that he would call her, and then he left with his ex-wife. Patricia felt like throwing up.

Betsy appeared in front of her. "Who was that with Steve?"

"His ex-wife."

"Oh no, not again."

Patricia's heart sank as Betsy put into words what she was trying very hard not to acknowledge. Steve had just walked out on her without even saying goodbye, to go somewhere with his ex-wife. She felt like bawling or throwing something.

But she didn't, she squared her shoulders. "He said he'd call me, so I'm not jumping to any conclusions until I hear from him. It was awesome having you at the summit Betsy, but I need to go help with the cleanup and tear down."

"I understand, call me if you need to talk. I'm here for you, if you need it. I'm driving back to Grand Junction tomorrow, but I have hands free calling and will be home this evening."

"Thanks, but I'll be fine. I'm sure he'll call in an hour or so and let me know what's up."

Betsy nodded. "I hope so."

∼

STEVE DIDN'T CALL IN AN HOUR OR EVEN THAT EVENING, but she chalked it up to travel. He didn't call the next day or even the whole week after the summit. She kept her phone with her at all times, even while she was lecturing. But he didn't call, he didn't text, and he didn't send her an email. She checked her phone constantly, she checked the news to make sure a plane hadn't crashed or a huge accident didn't happen in Virginia, she checked her email, she checked her mailbox, she checked her teacher box in the office, hell she even checked to make sure no carrier pigeons had landed. But there was nothing, not one damn word from him, even his Facebook account didn't have a peep from him.

Calling him was something she couldn't bring herself to do, although she came close a couple of times. Fear of him answering his phone when he was with his ex-wife kept her from pushing the send button. What a fool she'd been mouthing off about being fine, thinking she could just cut the cord and move on, what a bunch of crap. She'd give anything to have a chance, even at a long-distance relationship, but her phone didn't ring, Steve didn't call.

But she did get phone calls from Aaron. One afternoon on the second week after the summit was over she heard her phone ringing in her pocket, she was on her way up the hill to her house so she grabbed it, and answered without looking at who it was.

"You bitch, what lies did you tell to get me fired."

"What?" She looked at the caller display. "Aaron is that you? What are you talking about?"

"You know perfectly well, what I'm talking about. Coach Calhoun just fired me for sexual harassment of the female

166

professors. Since you're the only female professor I've had any trouble with, it had to be you."

"What do you mean had any trouble with?" she asked.

"I mean, Ice Princess, you're the only woman who didn't relish joining me in bed. The rest of them were not just a tease like you."

She huffed and she continued up the hill. "Well thank you for that enlightening bit of news, but I didn't say a word to anyone. I didn't see your comments as anything worthy to even mention, let alone file a complaint."

"Yeah right, you're lying through your teeth. What did you do, spy on me when I took those co-eds out, and get jealous?"

"What? You took students out? Students in your classes or on the track team?"

Aaron laughed, it was a nasty sound. "Yeah, so what's it to you, the girls were coming on to me. I didn't turn them down."

"You had sex with students you had authority over? That is wrong in so many ways, I can't begin to count them."

"Well you better not say anything about that to anyone, and the only reason you think it's wrong is because you're a frigid bitch."

"Hanging up now."

She heard him yelling as she pushed the end button. Her hands were shaking from the encounter but out of anger, not fear. She put her phone back in her pocket and every time her phone rang after that she checked who was calling and didn't answer it when she saw it was Aaron. He kept calling and leaving nasty messages, until she finally turned her phone off at midnight.

The calls started up the next day, but she put her phone on vibrate and deleted all the voice-mail messages without listening to them. None of the calls were from Steve and she didn't care to listen to Aaron's craziness.

When she'd heard someone in her yard late one night, she called the police. She didn't know if it was Aaron, but she wasn't taking any chances. The police didn't find anyone but there was spray paint on the side of her house, not a lot, so apparently the police had scared the person off.

The next morning, ten days after the summit she called her sister in Hawaii.

"Hello sister of mine," Diane answered perkily.

"Hi, Diane. So, spring break is next week, and I was thinking about coming to see you guys."

"That would be awesome, but won't you end up paying a fortune for tickets, on this short of notice?"

"Probably, but I don't really care what they cost. I need a change of scenery and some ocean time."

Then there was silence on the other end for a few seconds and then Diane said softly, "You haven't heard from Steve have you?"

"No, I have not, but that's not the only reason I'm coming." She didn't want to worry her sister, so she wasn't going to mention the phone calls from Aaron or the vandalism. Hopefully he would be gone by the time she got back from Hawaii. "I haven't seen the kids in a while, and I want to swim in the ocean. I want to get out of this fricken town, and I just don't give a crap how expensive it is. I need a break."

"Well you are always welcome to join us. I'll get the kids to clean up the guest room. They think it's their personal play room, there are toys everywhere. But they will be so happy that their auntie is coming they won't give me any trouble." Diane assured her.

"Good, I'm going to book the tickets for as soon as I can get out of town, after my last class Friday afternoon."

"Awesome, want us to pick you up, or do you want to rent a car?"

"I think I'll rent a car, that way I can be footloose and fancy free."

Diane said, "Okay then we'll see you when we see you."

CHAPTER 23

A few days later Patricia's plane was landing at the Kona airport when she heard a panicked voice behind her. "Oh no, we're landing in a lava field, is the pilot lost? Are we going to crash?"

Patricia chuckled to herself, it was a common reaction for people landing in the Kona airport for their first time, because it *was* in the middle of a lava field and all you could see out of one side of the plane was ocean and lava rock. The surface was bumpy and jagged and looked like it could tear your plane to bits. The 'A'ā lava flows on this part of the island looked kind of scary to a newbie, but the runway was smooth, so when the plane touched down, she heard the woman behind her sigh in relief.

Patricia just laughed as she put her duffle on her shoulder and walked out into the stream of people deplaning. There were two exits, one in the front and one in the back, so it was a relatively quick process, even if you did have to carry your bags down the stairs or ramp—and across the tarmac—to the cute little shack-looking terminal buildings. The wave of warm humid air hit her as she walked out of the air-cooled plane, she could practically hear her skin rejoice and suck in the moisture.

Once Patricia got away from the plane and jet fuel fumes, she took a deep breath and could smell the plumeria. Hawaii had its own unique scent, and the Kona airport being all outdoors made the experience of arriving special. She took the band out of her hair, shook her head, and decided to buy herself a lei, from one of the vendors. They were expensive here at the airport, but she wanted one, indulging herself this one time wouldn't break her budget.

She decided on a simple plumeria lei, with tiny pink carnations, in between the plumeria flowers. She'd been tempted by the pikake, with its delightful scent, but she wanted the fresher, subtler smell of the plumerias.

While she waited for her luggage, she slipped her shoes and socks off and put on some rubber flip-flops that people in Hawaii called slippers. She unzipped the bottom layer of her cargo pants and put them in her duffle along with her shoes, socks and hoodie. Leaving her in an orange tank top, if she'd had a tan she would blend right in, but her pale skin and her lei marked her as a tourist.

Once she had her luggage and rental car, she turned onto the highway, or what they called a highway in Kona, which was a normal road anywhere else. It was four lanes in some places and two lanes in others, with nothing dividing the two directions of traffic. She decided to drive along the shore, for the short five miles she could, so she turned off the Queen K Highway, onto Palani road, and then onto Ali'i drive. She would drive by the palace and the oldest church and then right next to the ocean.

It was so beautiful, her sister lived much further south, so she decided to quickly stop for some sushi at the tiny little place hidden in the back, off of Ali'i drive. It was a place that they made your sushi rolls fresh with whatever ingredients you wanted put in them. She loved the teriyaki chicken with cucumber and avocado. It was early enough, that there was only a couple people ahead of her, there were times when the line was out the door.

She got her sushi, a can of lilikoi juice and a bottle of water and went back to her car, heading down Ali'i drive to sit in the shade on one of the benches, at Pahoehoe park. It was a favorite place to sit and watch the waves roll in. Not a great place to get your feet wet, but she could do that later.

There was a bench in the shade next to the sea wall, where she could eat her lunch and watch the waves. Fish could be seen in the curl of the wave as it rushed to the shore, the water was clear and a beautiful turquoise blue. She didn't know how long she sat there, but her food was long gone, it was so peaceful, and she felt herself center and heal. She might miss Steve, but she wouldn't die without him, or from a broken heart as so many movies and books suggested. She would truly be fine, not perfect, but content.

Sighing, she stood up and stretched, she dreaded getting back in her car to drive south to her sister's house. It was only a few miles but this time of day the traffic could be horrible, it wasn't a school day though, so that would help. On school days, down near Kealakekua, you could walk faster than drive.

But she should get moving, she needed to get there in the daylight, it was darn dark out there in the coffee plantations when the sun set. Not that she was in any real danger of the sun setting, it was only mid-afternoon, but she was sure her sister had figured out what time she would be landing and would worry if it got too late.

She disposed of her trash and got in her red mustang convertible, nearly all the rental cars in Hawaii were convertibles, which were fine, if you didn't have much luggage. But for a family of four, it was a hoot watching them try to get all their luggage in the tiny trunk. There were also mini-vans, but who wanted one of those, when you could have the sun on your face and the wind blowing in your hair? She wondered how many people ended up taking the drop-tops back and trading them for a mini-van.

Less than an hour later, she pulled into her sister's driveway, and up to the house. She didn't even get the door shut on the car, before her niece and nephew came running out of the house and into her arms.

"You're here, Auntie," Brandon yelled as he wrapped his arms around her neck. He was the spitting image of his father with brown eyes and brown hair, and a brown body from hours spent outdoors playing on the plantation.

Patricia squeezed her nephew tight in a bear hug and kissed his cheek. "I am, I'm here just to see you two."

She turned to her niece. "Does auntie get a hug from you too, Brooke?"

Brooke nodded and stepped up for a less exuberant hug. She was adorable with long curling brown hair that was sun-streaked in gold. She had dark green eyes and a dimple in one cheek. "You two have grown so much since I was here last."

Brandon puffed out his chest and said, "I am six now, so I had to grow, last time you were here I was only five."

Patricia smiled; he'd just turned six a few weeks ago. "Yes, you couldn't stay little, with a new birthday. And how old are you now, Brooke?" She knew how old her niece was, but wanted to include her in the conversation, Brandon had such a force of character that Brooke was sometimes in his shadow, she was a quieter child.

Brooke held out four fingers and quietly said, "I'm four."

Patricia nodded. "And a very beautiful four."

Brooke smiled shyly. Patricia look back to Brandon when he grabbed her hand. "Mommy said to bring you inside when you got here, that she would send daddy out to get your things."

She laughed. "That's what daddies are for, I suppose, to carry heavy things." She held out her other hand to Brooke, who slipped her small hand into Patricia's and they headed toward the door. They paused to slip their shoes off at the door and then went into the house.

When they got inside Brandon started hollering at the top of his lungs. "Mommy, mommy, Auntie is here, she's here."

Diane came out from somewhere in the back of the house. It was a typical plantation style house, all on one level with wide eaves and plenty of windows that were open to let in the cooling breezes. The coffee plantation houses were single sided, with no insulation, the outer wall could be seen from the inside and you could see the studs for the walls running from floor to ceiling. The electricity was often in the floor-boards, which had the two layers normally seen in mainland construction. No insulation was needed, as the houses had the sea breezes to cool the house.

Diane said, "Yes I see that Brandon, but you don't need to shout the house down with the news. We all knew she would be here sometime soon."

"Yes mommy, but I didn't want you to miss her being here, now."

Diane smiled as she walked over to hug her sister. "Hard to argue with that logic. It's good to have you come for a visit. How was the traffic? Are you hungry?"

"Actually, that new bypass helps so much, the traffic was not bad at all. I stopped for some sushi and ate it at Pahoehoe, watching the waves roll in."

Diane grinned. "Ah, so that's why you wanted to rent a

car, so you could stop at your favorite sushi place on your way to my house. Did you have shaved ice too?"

"No, I thought we could take the kids for the treat." Brooke smiled when she heard that.

Brandon asked, "Do we get to go to Honoka'a for malasadas since Auntie is here? We always go for malasadas when she comes."

"We'll see."

"Oh, and to the beach? We must go to the beach. Black sands to see the turtles? I just love it when Auntie comes to visit, we do such fun things." Brandon's eyes were as big as saucers.

Patricia and Diane both laughed at the little boy's enthusiasm. Patricia smiled at him. "I'm sure we'll find plenty of things to do while I'm here."

"Auntie, auntie, we went to the store and bought your favorite juice do you want one?" Brandon said, taking her hand to start pulling her toward the fridge.

"No, I got a juice on my way to your house, we can save yours for later." She looked at her sister. "I might need a vacation, from my vacation, when I leave here."

Diane nodded. "Very possibly."

STEVE BREATHED A SIGH OF RELIEF, HE'D BEEN IN A FRANTIC and frightening situation for two weeks, and it was finally over. He had not had one single minute to call Patsy and explain, he hoped she would let him, after the long silence. When he'd left the summit, he hadn't really thought the situation was as dire as Katerina had said, she was always a bit of a drama queen, so he hadn't taken the time to explain to Patsy then, thinking he could call her when he got to Virginia. But no, Katerina had been right to be worried. In fact, she probably should have been even more worried, than she had been.

His ex-brother-in-law had scared the crap out of him, and he'd been afraid to leave him alone, long enough to make a phone call, even a short one. He had hardly slept or even showered in the two weeks he'd been back in Virginia. But finally, they had gotten through to Thomas. The counselors, doctors and physical therapists had all agreed they were finally out of the critical period. Thomas had a long way to go, but there was no longer any immediate danger.

They all believed he was no longer suicidal, and it would be safe to stop monitoring him. Steve was so darn glad he had rushed back with Katerina, because he was fairly certain Thomas would not be around, if he'd just been with his sister. Katerina did not have the emotional strength to pull her brother through.

He dialed Patsy's phone number and it went straight to voice mail. He didn't leave a message the first six times he called. He finally left one asking her—even begging her—to call him back.

CHAPTER 24

*P*atricia walked up the hill to her office. Spring break was over; she'd had a fun time in Hawaii with her sister and her family. Thank God the kids had kept her busy, so she couldn't dwell on her heartbreak. During the summit, she'd been so sure she could move past it quickly, but no, that wasn't happening.

It had been three weeks since Steve had left, and she still felt the loss, but she knew from experience she could go on and have a satisfying life. She wasn't going to try to convince herself she would find someone else, she had discovered she was a one-man woman, whether she liked it or not. But she could still have a pleasant time. Being in Hawaii had centered her and given her peace, she was determined to enjoy her solitary world.

She still had her job and her home and her family. She still loved to go into the mountains and take her students rock hounding and show them how to discover the origins of the area. She still had her volleyball team, and she loved to go to the school sporting events. She would miss Steve, but life would go on.

She walked into her office and dropped her backpack on the chair by the door. There was a large envelope on her desk, from the Bureau of Land Management. What was that for? It had her name and the school address on the front, but oddly enough, no postage. She opened it with the letter opener from the pencil holder on her desk and pulled out the pages. It was a claim for the area she and Steve had found. It had her name as the claim holder, and the mine was named *Always*.

She huffed, that man had some nerve, first he filed a claim in her name and then named it Always. Always what? Always alone? Always broken? Always leaving? Always someone else? No, for her, it would mean Always in her heart, whether he was with her or not, he was her one and only. As much as she wished it wasn't true, it was.

She shoved the claim and the envelope to the corner of her desk and turned on her computer. She was sure, she had a ton of emails to sort through, she hadn't even tried to look at them while she was in Hawaii, she had taken a whole week just to herself and had gloried in it. Today was soon enough to get back in touch with her job.

She saw one from the administration about a new professor, she clicked on it and Steve's face filled the screen. What? Steve the new professor? Surely not, he was back in Virginia with his ex-wife. She carefully read the email. As she read the words her mind whirled and she vaguely heard someone come in her outer office, probably her grad student Tracy.

"What kind of joke is this? Steve the new professor and track coach? When did this happen? What does this mean, what am I going to do?

"I hope you will marry me and have my babies." Steve's deep voice startled her.

"What? I thought you were back with your ex-wife." She demanded.

178

"Nope, I tried to call you to explain, but you didn't answer my calls."

"You did not call for two weeks, but Aaron did, ranting about me getting him fired. I had no idea what he was talking about, but it scared me, so I decided to get out of town. I went to Hawaii to see my sister, and my carrier has virtually no service where she lives on the Big Island. So, I always turn it off when I get there. It ran out of power and is currently on the charger at home because I packed it in my luggage, like an idiot, and then my damn flight was delayed last night, and I just didn't have the energy to deal with it when I finally got here." Her voice got shriller with each word until she was practically screeching, but she'd been through a lot in the last month. No thanks to the man standing in her office grinning at her.

"I missed you too. Oh, Patsy, my sweet love, I didn't go back to Virginia to be with my ex-wife, I told you that ship has sailed."

"But you did leave with her, and I saw her pleading with you, even with tears."

"Yes, you did. Her brother Thomas and his unit got hit by an IED, nearly everyone died almost instantly. He was bleeding badly from his leg being ripped apart, and the only other survivor got a tourniquet on him, so he didn't bleed out. Then they protected each other from the enemy gunfire, until help arrived. His friend died before they could get to a medical facility, he'd been gut shot, and her brother didn't know."

Steve paced across her office and turned back toward her. "Thomas lost his leg, but had such survivors guilt, Katerina was afraid he would kill himself. He wouldn't go to therapy, he wouldn't go to counseling, he wouldn't talk to her. She'd put him in a 48-hour watch facility and came to find me, to see if I could get through to him."

He ran his hands through his hair and gripped. "When I got there, he was totally closed off, but I just dragged him to his appointments. We didn't leave him alone for one minute, and finally after two weeks, he broke down and talked about it. He's still grieving, but he's going to his appointments and talking about living again. Once he turned the corner I tried to call, but your phone went straight to voice mail."

Steve shrugged. "So, I started wrapping up my life in Virginia and moved here. I put the house in Thomas's name, so he has somewhere to live, quit my job and got on the plane. I had already talked to the department head and Coach Calhoun about taking over the track and field team. I heard this morning that the department head wants me to do some freelancing on a mine they're having trouble with, in Spirit Lake, it's giving some rancher's a hard time."

She gasped when he got down on one knee. "I didn't want to live so far away from you. I love you and I want to spend the rest of my life with you. Will you marry me?"

Her throat closed and tears started streaming down her face. She couldn't say a word, she just stared at him. She couldn't believe this was happening, she was going to be able to spend her life with the man she loved, her one and only. He drew a ring box out of his pocket and opened it to the most beautiful aquamarine engagement ring. The center stone was an oval cut aquamarine surrounded by diamonds.

"It's from our claim. I had a jeweler start working on it the moment I got to Virginia. So, will you wear it and marry me."

She still couldn't speak; he'd made her a ring from their mine. It was so exactly perfect; he was so exactly perfect. She nodded and held out her left hand. He laughed and slipped the ring on her finger. Then he pulled her into his arms and kissed her long and hard.

EPILOGUE

*S*teve grinned as he slid the last brushful of paint on the house. Time for a cold beer. His friends were washing out their brushes and having a water fight in the back yard, far away from the newly painted house, while they waited for him to finish the trim on the little stop sign shaped window at the very top of the house.

When he was finished, they planned to kick back, have some brews and grill some meat. He'd specifically asked for them to help paint in lieu of a bachelor party. They'd all happily agreed to help him paint the house. The little attic window was the last thing to be painted and he'd wanted to do that finishing touch himself.

The house being painted was the last thing on Patsy's list of home repairs, she'd teased him with back during the energy summit in March. It had been an amazing six months and he was thrilled to be taking this next step.

That list of completed repairs was his surprise wedding gift to her. It had taken a lot of planning to get them all done without her being the wiser to his plan. He'd had to snoop through her browsing history to see what kind of bathroom sink she'd wanted, for the spare bathroom, as well as make several calls to her sister.

He'd casually asked what colors she would like to paint the house and was relieved when she'd mentioned she wanted basically the same color of slate blue it was, but with a tiny bit richer shade of blue and white trim.

They had already planted flowers for the summer, but she'd talked about wanting bulbs for the spring next year, that was a surprise she wouldn't know about for six months. It hadn't been easy to dig up the summer flowers, plant the bulbs and put the flowers back in, so she couldn't see he had done anything. But he'd accomplished it, with some suggestions from the gardening center.

He had another surprise for her that she hadn't asked for and no one else knew about, he'd taken the spare bedroom cum office and turned it into a nursery. She hadn't yet told him she was pregnant, but he knew she was. He suspected it was going to be his surprise wedding gift, and he couldn't be happier about that idea.

He'd looked through her browser history and had seen some baby room décor in her list of favorite links. So, he'd spent a small fortune on all the things they had in the store, that matched the theme she'd picked out, and the room was awesome. He'd done the project all by himself without any help from his friends. The only thing he was slightly worried about, was if she wanted to do it herself. He'd thought about asking Diane, but had nixed that idea quickly, if Patsy had not yet told her, he didn't want to ruin the surprise.

But the hardest piece of all had been getting her out of the house, he and her sister had to do some fast talking to convince her to go to a spa for the week before the wedding. He'd wanted a whole week, but she'd balked at that, and they'd finally managed to talk her into three days. It had been a challenge to get everything done in three short days, but he'd gotten it all finished and was quite proud of himself.

The wedding was tomorrow, and she would be spending the last night in Estes Park where the wedding was scheduled. She'd picked a beautiful outdoor location with the Rocky Mountains in the background and a lovely stream running next to the chapel. They would have the chapel to change clothes in, and they could all cram inside it, if the weather didn't cooperate. But the forecasters were calling for clear skies and warm temperatures.

The grounds had a pretty arch they could get married under and it was surrounded by red sandstone, similar to what could be seen at Red Rocks, so she would be married surrounded by her beloved rocks. It was perfect for her and he was happy with it as well.

"Hey Sampson, quit your daydreaming and get your butt down here, so we can start grilling." Thomas his ex-brother-in-law yelled up at him. Steve had called to tell him his good news, and Thomas had threatened him with death if he wasn't invited to the wedding, so of course he was invited, and he'd done a good job painting the lower levels. He had a prosthesis now and was quite steady on it. They didn't let him climb any ladders, but that was about the only concession he'd needed.

Steve waved and started down the ladder, he was a very happy man, in a little less than twenty-four hours he would be married to the love of his life, and they would be starting their lives and a family together.

He collapsed the ladder down to carrying size, stepped back with it, to look at the house where he would spend the rest of his life and grinned, it was going to be a great adventure.

The End

THE HELLUVA ENGINEER SERIES CONTINUES WITH CHRISTMAS at the Rockin' K where the Kipling family is having trouble with water contamination from a suspected gold mine in the hills above the ranch. Steve and Patricia take their interns with them to investigate, while the Kipling family gathers to celebrate the Holidays.

If you enjoyed this story, please leave a review on your favorite retailer, Bookbub, or Goodreads.
Thanks so much!

BURLAP AND BARBED WIRE SERIES

SADDLES AND SECRETS SERIES

Wyoming Wranglers

The Lawman: Saddles and Secrets #1

Maggie Ann and John's story

The Watcher: Saddles and Secrets #2

Christina and Rob's story

The Rescuer: Saddles and Secrets #3

Milly and Tim's story

The Vacation: Saddles and Secrets Short Story #4

Andrea and Carl Ray's story

(Part of the Getting Wild in Deadwood anthology)

The Neighbor: Saddles and Secrets #5

Terri and Rafe's story

HELLUVA ENGINEER SERIES

Helluva Engineer: Helluva Engineer #1

Patricia and Steve's story

Christmas at the Rockin' K: Helluva Engineer #2

Brenda and Thomas's story

ABOUT THE AUTHOR

What does a geeky math nerd know about writing romance?

That's a darn good question. As a former techy I've done everything from computer programming to international trainer. Prior to college I had lots of different jobs and activities that were so diverse, I was an anomaly.

None of that qualifies me for writing novels. But I have some darn good stories to tell and a lot of imagination.

I have lived in Colorado, Hawaii and currently reside in Washington. Going from two states with 340 days of sun to a state with 340 days of clouds, I had to do something to perk me up. And that's when I started this new adventure called author. Joining the Romance Writers of America and two local chapters, helped me learn the craft quickly and was a ton of fun.

My family consists of two grown children, their spouses, two adorable grand-daughters, and one grand dog. My favorite activity is playing with my granddaughters!

When the girls can't play with their amazing grand-mother, my interests are reading and writing, yay! I started reading at a young age with the Nancy Drew mysteries and have continued to be an avid reader my whole life. My favorite reading material is romance, but occasionally if other stories creep into my to-be-read pile, I don't kick them out.

Some of the strange jobs I have held are a carnation grower's worker, a trap club puller, a pizza hut waitress, a software engineer, an international trainer, and a business program manager. I took welding, drafting and upholstery in high school, a long time ago, when girls didn't take those classes, so I have an eclectic bunch of knowledge and experience.

And for something really unusual... I once had a raccoon as a pet.

Join with me as I tell my stories, weaving real tidbits from my life in with imaginary ones. You'll have to guess which is which. It will be a hoot!

Contact me:

www.shirleypenick.com
To sign up for Shirley's Monthly Newsletter, sign up on my website or send email to shirleypenick@outlook.com, subject newsletter.

Follow me:

facebook.com/ShirleyPenickAuthorFans

twitter.com/shirley_penick

instagram.com/shirleypenickauthor

bookbub.com/authors/shirley-penick

goodreads.com/shirleypenick

Made in the USA
Coppell, TX
05 January 2022

70809208R00108